The Outrage at the Diogenes Club

[Being another manuscript found in the tin dispatch box of
Dr John H. Watson
in the vault of Cox & Co., Charing Cross, London]

Book Four in the Series,
Sherlock Holmes and the American Literati

As Edited

By

Daniel D. Victor, Ph.D.

Paperback ISBN 978-1-78092-678-0
ePub ISBN 978-1-78092-679-7
PDF ISBN 978-1-78092-812-8

Published in the UK by MX Publishing
335 Princess Park Manor, Royal Drive,
London, N11 3GX
www.mxpublishing.co.uk

Cover design by www.staunch.com

Also by Daniel D. Victor

The Seventh Bullet:
The Further Adventures of Sherlock Holmes

A Study in Synchronicity

The Final Page of Baker Street
(Book One in the series,
Sherlock Holmes and the American Literati)

Sherlock Holmes
and the
Baron of Brede Place
(Book Two in the series,
Sherlock Holmes and the American Literati)

Seventeen Minutes to Baker Street
(Book Three in the series,
Sherlock Holmes and the American Literati)

Here's another for Norma, Seth, and Ethan

Acknowledgements

Thanks and appreciation to Norma Silverman, Judy Grabiner, Sandy Cohen, Mark Holzband, and Barry Smolin for all their help and inspiration.   Thank you to Rory Lalwan, Senior Archives & Local Studies Assistant, City of Westminster Archives Centre, for clarifying some issues about London's libraries. And a special thanks to David Marcum for not only making suggestions about the text, but also for supplying the proverbial "kick in the pants" to get me started in the first place.

An easy but erroneous assumption would be that there were no loose ends, no unanswered questions. Yet, as with any conspiracy, more than a few still linger.

--Thomas A. Bogar
Backstage at the
Lincoln Assassination

Murder is a tawdry little crime; it's born of greed, or lust, or liquor. Adulterers and shopkeepers get murdered. But when a president gets killed, when Julius Caesar got killed—he was assassinated.

--John Weidman
Spoken by the character,
John Wilkes Booth,
in *Assassins*

The best government is a benevolent tyranny tempered by an occasional assassination.

--Voltaire (attributed)

As previously, while the following manuscript appears as Dr Watson wrote it, I have taken the liberty to give his narrative a title, separate it into sections, and introduce his chapters with what I hope are relevant headnotes from the works of Jack London.

D.D.V.
November 2016

Chapter One

No other book of mine [*The People of the Abyss*]
took so much of my young heart and tears
as that study of the economic degradation of the poor.
--Jack London
Letter to George Sterling

In looking backward, I have come to recognise the irresponsible nature of my reporting. I could not possibly have been more naïve. However prescient a writer I may have regarded myself, I never anticipated that some purveyor of evil might take advantage of the information I had so innocently provided in public print. I refer, of course, to my primary narratives involving Mr Mycroft Holmes: "The Greek Interpreter" and "The Bruce-Partington Plans".

Critics as well as supporters of those sketches should rightly denounce my self-deception. I never stopped to consider the ramifications. I never imagined miscreants so vile as to convert the details from my accounts into a devious scheme to dispatch the invaluable Mycroft—though "assassinate" seems the more relevant verb.

How unassuming of me! Not only did I reveal to England's enemies the indispensable nature of his link to the British government, but I even went so far as to announce his daily schedule. I readily confess my culpability. The blame for the outrage that occurred at the Diogenes Club should fall entirely upon me. I was the one who set the machinery in motion.

It was upon a cool and dark summer's day in 1902 that Sherlock Holmes and I first became acquainted with the sinister force that would eventually target his brother. And yet it must be said that at the time Holmes himself first heard of the threat, he failed to take it seriously. Quite the contrary. He joined me in laughing at the proposition.

*****

By August of '02, I had vacated our old rooms in Baker Street and moved into my own digs. Separated as Holmes and I now were, we had to co-ordinate our professional engagements in advance. Readers familiar with the narrative I called "The Illustrious Client" may remember a discussion we had in the drying room of Nevill's Turkish Bath during the morning of Wednesday, the third of September in '02. It was at Nevill's that Holmes invited me to a meeting later that day in Baker Street.

To be more precise, the well-connected Sir James Damery was coming round at half-four; and my friend reckoned that a case was in the offing. At the time, of course, Holmes had no inkling that Damery's words would trigger our inquiry into the dealings of the ruthless Baron Adelbert Gruner. On the contrary, given Sir James' list of high-ranking acquaintances, Holmes believed the matter would concern some delicate social issue that wanted cleaning up.

Now any such invitation from Sherlock Holmes was enough to motivate me; but include a whiff of scandal, and the appeal became irresistible. I immediately agreed to stop in at 221B later that day.

In the aforementioned "The Illustrious Client", I detailed Sir James' concerns, and I need not repeat them here. Suffice it to say, the matter was anything but trivial. Miss Violet de Merville, a young lady in distress, required immediate aid. So upset was Sir James, in fact, that Holmes himself, after bidding farewell to his distinguished guest, quickly exited the flat. He was off to find the underworld agent called Shinwell Johnson who he believed could provide necessary informants.

"Dinner at 8.00!" Holmes did manage to shout up to me as he dashed down the stairs. "At Simpson's!"

*****

With no reason to return to my own residence before joining Holmes, I decided to remain in Baker Street to take up the "professional business" to which I referred in "The Illustrious Client". In point of fact, I wanted to evaluate the remaining medical files I had left in my room. Fortunately, the review took but half an hour, and I decided to spend the time I had left relaxing in the sitting room with a copy of the *Telegraph*.

Settling into my familiar velvet-lined armchair in front of a warming fire, I fully intended to read the newspaper. I must have dozed off, however; for all I can remember was starting dramatically at a crisp knock at the door.

"Yes?" I managed to say.

The door opened; and in the few moments it took to brush aside the cobwebs, I realised that, with no Sherlock Holmes present to receive any callers, it was to me that the boy in buttons was announcing the arrival of a man come to see the consulting detective.

"Jack London," muttered Billy the page, darting a suspicious glance behind him at the caller so named. Not only had Billy's voice harboured an unusual note of disdain, but also the omission of the title, "Mister".

Jack London? I remember thinking. *Means nothing to me—curious, though, in a metropolis of the same name. I wonder if it might not be some sort of mercurial pseudonym based on whatever city the man finds himself in.* Perhaps, he's Jack Manchester *in the north.*

Billy's lacklustre introduction was immediately followed by a prolonged look of disgust as the lad backed away to make room for the visitor. Billy actually pressed himself flat against the open door to avoid being so much as accidentally brushed by the stranger. What's more, once the man had entered, the boy wasted no time in beating a hasty retreat.

It took but a moment to comprehend Billy's odd behaviour. A darting look at the man's tattered clothing served well enough to brand him a vagrant. No need for me to recall Holmes' admonition about checking someone's cuffs or knees to intuit his background.

The man's entire ensemble trumpeted poverty. A dark jacket, perhaps originally navy-blue, revealed frayed cuffs and worn elbows; a hole in the tan trousers exposed the right knee; and one of his brown brogues, scuffed almost white, looked to be coming apart at an inner seam. His left hand, its knuckles marred by scars and discolouration, held a well-worn flat cap of indistinguishable tweed. And if his sorry state was not apparent enough, an unsavoury aroma of stale tobacco and old garbage, the stink of the street, underscored the point. In short, the man reeked; and the heat from the fireplace made the stench all the worse.

This embodiment of penury belonged to a pale-faced young man in his early twenties. A nest of dishevelled dark hair sat atop his crown, and his narrow blue eyes glanced furtively about the room. With his lips tightly closed, he could offer only the faintest hint of a smile.

On the street, one might not take a second look at such a figure; and due to my criminal investigations with Holmes, I had grown used to all sorts of strange people who appeared at Baker Street. Yet there was something irregular about this caller that raised my suspicions. For instance, his dress looked threadbare though he himself did not appear to be starving; and in spite of his nervous fidgeting and self-conscious shifting from one leg to the other, his broad shoulders and erect bearing suggested a man who could fend for himself.

It is from just such contradictory characteristics that questions of disguise come to mind. For a moment I entertained the idea that the visitor might be Sherlock Holmes himself. Though the caller stood about five-foot-seven inches tall and my friend well over six feet, I had known Holmes to mask even such differences as height.

As I re-examined the visitor, however, I observed no stooping in his stature; and his rough hands seemed genuine enough. What's more, with his upright stance and feet set wide apart, a new image popped into my head—that of a deckhand on the high seas. I envisioned the rolling ship and—

An American-accented voice brought me back to reality. "I'm looking for Sherlock Holmes," said the stranger.

As soon as he opened his mouth to speak, I could see why he kept his lips pressed together: He had no front teeth. *Probably knocked out in a fight somewhere—on a ship, no doubt.* To me, the gap made him look pugnacious; and yet I could well imagine more sympathetic types—nurturing women, in particular—envisioning a cute little boy behind the toothless smile. The tousled hair and questioning eyes added to the portrait of a young child in need of mothering.

"Mr Holmes isn't in," said I, keeping my distance. "I'm his friend and colleague, Dr Watson. You may rest assured that whatever you have to say to Mr Holmes you may say to me, and I'll pass it along to him."

The man looked me up and down. "You're Dr Watson? Dr *John* Watson—the fellow who writes all those adventures about Sherlock Holmes?"

A blush crossed my face. I cannot help myself when my sketches evoke recognition. "Yes," said I, "the very same."

The visitor extended his hand, exposing a palm ridged with callosities. "Glad to meet you. I've read lots of your stories. Really good."

I had no choice. I was forced to take his hand, and he pumped mine several times. "I'm a writer too," said he.

Another American writer? 221B, it seemed, had become quite the literary *salon.* In point of fact, during the past few years, Holmes and I had encountered a number of authors from the States, but I must say that in spite of our first-hand familiarity with luminaries like Sam Clemens, Henry James, Graham Phillips, and the late Stephen Crane, I had never heard the name "Jack London" before.

"'A *writer',* you say?" The crackling fire failed to conceal the scepticism in my voice. "And just what is it that you *write*, Mr London?"

His face brightened as soon as he began discussing his work. "I mainly write short stories. My first book, *The Son of the Wolf,* was published a couple of years ago. It's a collection of my tales about the search for gold in the Yukon."

"Sorry," said I coldly, "never heard of it." I was not proud of my attitude that day, but another glance at the shabby state of his clothing had prompted me to speak with altogether too much directness. Even as I discounted his work aloud, I was thinking, *Probably published by some no-account little press.*

"Oh," said Jack London, the flickering light from the grate reflected in his narrow eyes, "*I* get it. Don't think I didn't see you giving me the once over. 'Cause of my rags and tatters, you think I can't possibly be a writer, eh? I must be on the doss—some bum who wandered off the street to beg for money or food or something. I certainly couldn't be on the same level as you."

Though I turned red-faced again, this time at being called out for my prejudice, I cannot say that I cared for his tone. And he was not yet finished hectoring me.

"Lemme tell you where I've just come from, Doctor—the 'ghetto', as some call the East End. Out there, you know, there are many poor folks who really *could* do with a hand-out. You know, some bread or a few pence. People are in a bad way."

Whether or not I had accurately been singled out as a snob, I was not certain. I did know that the East End was rife with desperate people. In fact, I had a vague memory of Holmes warning me never to go unarmed if traveling east of Aldgate. Even so, I did not enjoy being lectured to by the likes of this vagabond, and I was about to say so when he shifted the subject.

"Let's get back to your friend, Holmes."

"I told you, he's out."

London looked nervously round the room again. "No one else here?"

"No, my good man. We're quite alone."

"You're sure?"

"*Quite* sure."

9

"OK, then," said he, still shifting from one foot to the other, "I guess *you'll* have to do."

Normally, I would insist that a prospective client return when Holmes was present. But thanks to our earlier meeting with Sir James, I understood Holmes to have his hands full in dealing with the vile Baron Gruner. More to the point, I desired to be done with this arrogant fellow as quickly as I could, and I reckoned that eliciting his story might be the best way to accomplish the goal.

"Just what is it you want, sir?" I asked.

"Actually, Dr Watson," said he, his tone more civil now, "I'm writing a book about the poor wretches who live in the East End—'the people of the abyss,' I call 'em. That's why I'm dressed like this. I live among 'em, and I write of their horrors. It's deceptive, I know—posing as a seaman who's lost his kit and his money. You see, even though I really *am* a sailor, the part about losing all my stuff's made-up."

A self-confessed hypocrite, I thought. At least, I was right about the sea.

"Unlike the poor souls I'm writing about," he explained, "*I* can leave the doss-house whenever the feeling strikes me. Then it's just a short walk back to my own room. I'm staying in respectable a place not six doors away from the man who secured it for me. I was given his name at Thomas Cook and Son—you know, Cook's Tours. They told me to see a detective called 'Johnny Upright'. "

"Johnny Upright." Remarkably, I knew the name—an alias belonging to William Thick, a retired Metropolitan detective. Known for his upright posture and smart checked suits, Thick achieved a singular notoriety some fifteen years earlier. He had been falsely accused of being Jack the Ripper. Needless to say, there was no legitimacy to the claim; and by way of defence, he received the highest praise from Scotland Yard.

Whether Jack London knew of his host's past I had no clue. But London did pause a moment to reflect on the man. "You know," he chuckled, "it's kind of ironic when you come to think about it—I mean, meeting with a detective and then coming all the way across town to see Sherlock Holmes."

"Indeed. And also a bit convenient—having your own pleasant room, I mean, amidst all the squalor that you rail about."

London nodded. "Agreed. But I'm only the messenger; I'm just publicising the story. I already admitted that keeping a hideout like that is unfair. But first I have to take care of myself. So, yeah, while the other woebegones are starving, I have a little extra food and somewhere safe to sleep. I've even sewn a few coins into the lining of my jacket in case times get really tough and I can't get back to Johnny's."

"And for what reason, pray, are you putting yourself through all this?"

Jack London formed his closed-lipped smile. "Why, I intend to educate the world to the terrible plight of the oppressed. The social order needs to learn how the economic masters, the industrial magnates—we call 'em 'Robber Barons' in the States—are mistreating the poor."

Oh, dear! And I thought I was moving matters along. I should have suspected: the man's just another Socialist ranting about the exploitation of the proletariat.

Lest I be misunderstood, dear reader, allow me to point out that my sympathies extend to all the downtrodden peoples of the Empire. I have, in fact, broken bread with many a liberal-minded thinker who has worried about the citizens of the East End in particular. H.G. Wells is but one example. I had met him during Christmas time some two years before at Brede Place, Stephen Crane's old manor house. Wells' novel, *The Time Machine,* reported that these very same wretches, the inhabitants of the East End, "live in such artificial conditions as practically to be put off from the natural surface of the earth."

But then I required no Bertie Wells—not to mention this fellow Jack London—to remind me of such awful conditions. *I* appreciated well enough that I was enjoying the warmth of a fire whilst others could not. There are limits to charity, however. The poor must learn to stand on their own instead of blaming their misfortunes on the upper classes, let alone on sympathetic people like me.

The luckless of our society may benefit from my tolerance, but it does not follow that their defenders do. Once people like this man London start orating, they frequently have a difficult time turning off the spigot. Besides, truth be told, I had little doubt that the American radical standing before me had long since recognised that there was money to be made from his putative literary project.

One can be certain that compassionate audiences would long to hear from him. Why, to this day, our society remains filled with well-intentioned types willing to offer their hard-earned money for tales about the abject poor in order to learn how to help them. Nor can we forget the countless number of readers who seek what the Germans call *Schadenfreude*—that is, taking pleasure in the misery of others. Forget altruism! From where I stood, it seemed clear that Jack London's book about East End poverty would have no deficiency of buyers.

And yet the question persisted: what could this man possibly want with my friend and colleague? Unless I put the query directly to him, I could envision the remainder of a restful afternoon being consumed by long-winded speeches promoting socialism and even anarchy.

"Why do you desire to speak with Sherlock Holmes?" I demanded.

He smiled again; it was really more of a smirk.

"I was party to a conversation this morning that I thought Mr Holmes might be interested in." As he spoke, he moved closer to the fireplace. "It has to do with murder—more than one, in fact."

"Murder?" I repeated. "And just where did this conversation take place?"

"The Salvation Army barracks."

"And where exactly are they?"

"You don't know?" he snorted derisively. "Guess I'm not surprised. What cause would anybody living near Regent's Park have to know about the barracks?"

How many more insults do I have to suffer?

Perhaps he sensed my growing irritation. At any rate, having sidled up to bearskin hearthrug, he began to explain.

"First, let me tell you what I was doing there. Food's always scarce in the East End, and some fella I was working with yesterday told me you can get a free breakfast at the barracks. So early this morning—you have to be there before 7.00 if you wanna eat—I left my room and trekked down St. James's Street, along Pall Mall, past Trafalgar Square and on to the Strand."

"Surely, there's no Salvation Army in the Strand."

"Hold your horses," he said. "First, you have to cross the bridge."

"Waterloo?"

He nodded. "Then, when you reach Blackfriars Road, it's right near the Surrey Theatre—you, know, the music hall. That's where the peg is."

"The 'peg'?" To me, the word conveyed a place to hang one's hat; this man seemed to be speaking a foreign language.

"The *peg*. The *barracks*. The peg's what they call any place you can get a free meal. Maybe the word needs defining in my own book as well. Look for it in Chapter Eleven."

Typical American, I thought, *ever the salesman.* Still, he had my attention; and I asked, "It was at this 'peg' that you first heard talk of murder?"

He nodded, yet I must have sounded particularly sceptical when I asked, "Why not take your story to Scotland Yard then?"

"I did—not that I'm one to cosy up to coppers. But it seemed like a story the police should know about. So I talked to some Inspector—a tall, blond fella—"

"Gregson?" I ventured, recognising the flaxen hair.

"Right, Gregson it was—not that it matters. I finished telling him what I'd learned about these murders, and he calls over another dick, a rat-faced little guy with a French-sounding name—"

"Lestrade."

"Right again. Anyway, this Gregson tells the other one my story, and Lestrade looks me up and down, shakes his head and says, 'Conspiracy nutter.'

"'By Jove, you're right,' says Gregson with a laugh."

I could not agree more with the two Yarders, but I kept my thoughts in check.

"*Cops!* I've had my fill of 'em. Here or back in California—they're all the same. But then I started thinking about Sherlock Holmes. From what I've read about him in your stories, Doctor—how he faced down Professor Moriarty, in particular—I reckoned he might be just the fella to give me a fair hearing. I figured if anybody could, he'd be the one to make good use of what I'd heard."

"Tell *me* what you wanted to tell Holmes," said I, "and you can be sure he'll get the details."

Jack London shrugged his shoulders. "Why not? At least, I can get it off my *own* back anyway. The more people who hear the story, the more I can quit looking over my shoulder for somebody trying to shut me up."

A paranoiac as well. A splendid way to pass the time.

Even as Jack London had been warming himself by the fire, we had been standing face to face. Against my better judgement, I indicated the soft chair by the hearth opposite my

16

own. Let the foul smell sink into *Holmes'* chair. After all, it wasn't *I* the man had come to see.

London settled in and began again. "Here's the long and the short of it. You can believe it or not. That's *your* business."

I nodded and, filling my pipe with Arcadia mixture, leaned back in my chair. It was time to listen to what this distrustful, radical-thinking, self-proclaimed social critic had to say.

Chapter Two

There are things greater than our wisdom, beyond our justice.
The right and wrong of this we cannot say,
and it is not for us to judge.
  --Jack London
  "An Odyssey of the North"

Once begun, Jack London warmed to his narrative, employing his hands to aid explanation and his eyes to convey intensity. And yet, though obviously a natural storyteller, he remained unable to prevent his political asides from creeping in.

"For breakfast at the Barracks, the well-fed authorities offer the starving poor this swill they call 'skilly'."

I cocked an eyebrow at the term.

"It's a thin brew of oatmeal. They give you a pint of the stuff along with a six-ounce loaf of bread—*stale* bread."

"At least it's food," I felt the need to point out. "And *gratis.*"

"Sort of," London scoffed. "When this so-called breakfast is over, they make you put in time cleaning up the place. That's the way you pay for your meal."

Ungrateful as well, I thought, but held my tongue.

19

"When we finished our spells," he continued, "we all joined up out on the street. Naturally, such a motley crowd attracts the coppers, and a couple of 'em were walking back and forth eyeing the likes of us. You know how that lot look at the poor. To the cops, the ill-fed and ill-clothed are nothing but anarchists, fanatics or madmen. But, you see, I'm a writer and wasn't hankering for trouble, so I moved on down the street a bit.

"That's when I saw this gaunt old geezer propped up on a wooden bench. I remembered seeing him inside the barracks when we were eating, but out here he was wheezing and coughing. He was dressed in rags like everybody else, and he didn't look so good. Not healthy, if you know what I mean."

"Couldn't you ask the people in charge—the police you mentioned—to fetch a doctor?"

London laughed. He didn't dignify my question with an answer.

"This wrinkled old man—maybe he was fifty though he looked older, wasted—motions me over and grabs my hand. 'I need someone to talk to,' he says in a whisper. Well, I'm hoping to learn as much as I can for the book I'm writing, and he actually sounded like he'd had an education. So I sat down next to him. He was all skin and bones, and I could easily have pulled my hand out of his frail fingers, but instead I let him hold on to me.

"'What do you want?' I asked.

"'I've done some bad things in my day, mate,' he says in a weak voice, 'and I need someone to tell them to. I don't know how much time I've got left 'pon this earth to clear my conscience.' His voice was an echo of a rasp, and it was all I could do to hear him.

"'Why me?' I asked.

"He shrugged. 'I saw you nosing round in the barracks. You look like you want to learn things; you seem like you'd understand.'

"He'd pegged me right, and I nodded. Then he took a couple of quick breaths and told me his story."

Here London paused and looked about the room again. "You sure there's no one else in here that can listen in?"

I told him I was the only one there—and that no one was hiding in the hallway or upstairs in the bedrooms either.

He peered round once more and muttered, "OK, then," and repeated to me what the fellow had told him: "'You wouldn't know it from the state I'm in today,' the old man says, 'but I used to work for a high-class syndicate. The Assassination Bureau, Limited, it's called; and they pay good money for people like me.'

"'What do you mean, "people like me"?' I asked. 'What *are* you?'

"The old man pulled me closer. I could smell his foul breath. 'I'm an assassin,' he whispered, 'or *was*. I was paid to kill people.'

"I must say that the geezer got my interest up. But I had to wait for him to complete a tired cough before he began again.

"'From what I've been hearing,' he said, 'the Bureau's still run by a Russian fellow with lots of money. I don't know his name, but he supposedly lives here in London with his daughter who's yet a teen. People say the wife's dead. I believe he's been in charge for some ten years now.' Suddenly, his sharp eyes locked on mine. 'You're American, right?'

"I nodded, and he said, 'Well, don't think you're immune to these people just 'cause you're a Yank. I've been told the Bureau was going strong in America long before the Russian ever took over. By now, it's set up across the Channel as well.'

"The old man paused. We both saw the two coppers moving in our direction. Why should we worry? All we were guilty of was sitting on a bench.

"'I told you the organisation eliminates people,' the man went on, 'but it isn't the way you think. They don't just kill *anyone*; they have a conscience. They only target subjects the Bureau considers enemies of the public good—you know the type—corrupt rulers, crooked business magnates, vicious criminals, and the like.'"

"Hold on," I said to Jack London. "Do you mean to say that this *Bureau*, as you call it, sits in judgement regarding who should live and who should die?" If this were actually the case, then Jack

London's story did indeed sound like something that would interest Sherlock Holmes.

"I asked the old man the same," said London, "about sitting in judgement, I mean. After all, murder is murder.

"'Don't ask *me* to justify what the Bureau does!' he cries, pulling his hand away. 'I was just a hired gun.'"

London's tale defied credibility. If such an organisation really did exist, how come we had heard nary a word about it? At the very least, there would have been rumours.

"You've never heard of the Assassination Bureau," said London as if reading my mind, "because they have all sorts of clever ways to cover up what they do. At least, that's what the old man said. He told me that maybe their victims are killed by an expert assassin who gets away. Or maybe by a poor innocent that the Bureau is able to set up and take the fall. Or maybe their victims appear to die of natural causes. *You're* a doctor. *You* know how deadly some germs can be—and undetectable."

"Germs?" I repeated in disbelief. "Do you mean using microbes as weapons? Good heavens, man, no civilised person could stoop so low!"

London smiled at my *naiveté*. "The old man said, 'All that matters is that the murder can't be traced back to the syndicate. Planning a safe strategy may take a while,' he cautioned, 'but in the end, they always get their man—or woman.'

23

"After this last bit," reported London, "the old man leaned back against the bench. He looked winded, tired out. For a moment his eyes fluttered and then shut. It was at that instant that one of the two policemen swooped in.

"'Hoy!' shouted the copper, banging the old man's skinny legs with a dark, wooden club. '*You* know the law! Swine like you can't be sleeping on these benches!'

"The old man jerked awake, wincing and rubbing his thigh. His upper leg looked no broader than his lower arm.

"I was about to protest; but the copper with the club pointed the thing in my face, and I guess I was wise enough to keep my mouth shut.

"The two coppers moved on, laughing. I was enraged by these pawns of the ruling class, and yet I confess that I was thinking more about this man's fantastical story than about any anger I was harbouring. I waited for the cops to get far enough away, and then I asked my companion the inevitable question: 'who did *you* ever kill?'

"'*Me?*' His rheumy eyes opened wide at the memory, and for the first time he managed the beginnings of a smile. 'I got my feet wet in an attempt on the Queen—that last try in '82.'

"'*Last?*'

"He nodded slowly—as if the movement required great effort. 'There were at least eight tries on Victoria that I know of; maybe there were more.'"

I myself had heard of some of these attempts, but I never kept a tally. Upon *eight* occasions someone had tried to take the life of the Sovereign! *My word!*

"'The Bureau tried many different approaches' or so the old man maintained. 'At one time or another, they enlisted a bartender, a hunchback, even a group of Irish-American radicals called the Dynamitards. But no one could ever get it right—not even with thirty pounds of grade-A dynamite brought over from New York. And, of course, it didn't work out when I was involved either.

"'I was a young man back then, and all I had to do was hold the horses while a concealed gunman shot at the Queen as she was leaving Windsor Station. He fired at the precise moment another gunshot went off. My mate missed; but just like it had been planned, the other shooter, Robert Maclean, got the blame. You've probably heard of the lunatic Maclean. No? Somehow, the Bureau had secretly persuaded him to take a shot. He missed too, of course; but because he'd fired at her in public when she was entering her carriage—just as he'd been instructed to do—the police were able to nab him. One shooter was sufficient as far as they were concerned, and the true assassin and I got away.'

"I shook my head in disbelief, but the old man offered other examples for confirmation.

"'It was similar to the plan they used to assassinate your President Garfield,' he said. "Remember that nutter Charlie Guiteau who was charged with killing him at a train station in Washington? Oh, Guiteau did the shooting all right, but who it was that put him up to it and who it was that caused Garfield's medical treatment to be so badly botched was never revealed. The real killers escaped.'"

Jack London fixed me with his eyes. "I tell you, Dr Watson, my blood ran cold. I couldn't believe what the man was telling me. I had heard of this fella Guiteau, though I wasn't familiar enough with what he'd actually done to raise any questions about the details. I knew it was a sad affair—that Garfield had grand ideas about helping people and that he'd crossed a powerful Senator named Conkling in the process and that it took the President weeks to die. But . . . ."

London's voice trailed off, and his brow began to furrow. "Still, I'm a thinker and was quite prepared to ask the old man a larger question—"

"Which was?"

London managed a close-lipped smile. "Why, the same one *you* want to ask: Just who was behind it all? Just who exactly thought they could order the death of Queen Victoria and President Garfield and get away with it?"

London was right. He had indeed stated the same question I would have posed.

"The old man shook his head when I asked him. 'Not my worry, was it?' he answered with a ropey laugh. 'Somebody pays for a contract. The Bureau's administrative board decides if the case is ethical. That's how it worked with McKinley in New York as well.'

"'Go on,' I said to the old man. 'Everyone knows that McKinley was shot by an anarchist, a fella named Golgosh or Gulgosh . . . .'

"'Czolgosz,' the old man chuckled. 'Leon Frank Czolgosz— once again, just as the Bureau had planned it. All I can say on the matter is that other guns besides his were drawn that day.'"

"Really!" I exclaimed. To London—or to the old man he was quoting—the whole world seemed involved in some ridiculous sort of grand conspiracy. No one in his right mind could accept such a story as anything but nonsense. To do otherwise would mean to believe that virtually every assassination in the recent past was performed by this single diabolical organisation. The proposition was absurd.

"'So what happened to *you*?'" Jack London said he had asked the old man. "'How did you lose *your* job?'

"'I got old. Over the years, I killed an MP and a local gangster—nobody a Yank like you would ever have heard of. But then I started missing my marks, and the syndicate wanted to get rid of me. Brought in new blood, didn't they? Even some women—like the Russian's daughter.

"'One can only laugh. *New* blood. Sooner or later, they'll all learn what I learned. The syndicate's not an outfit you can walk away from. I had to hide out here in London Town. The Bureau's high-class; they don't come round the East End much.'

"Here the old man sighed and leaned back against the bench. He looked worn down. I figured he was pretty much talked out."

London took a deep breath himself, seemingly relieved at having completed the tale. "I didn't know what to make of the old man," said he, "—whether to believe him or not, I mean. I wished him well and said I hoped he felt better for sharing his story. He nodded in my direction, thanked me for listening, and closed his eyes once more. I started off along Blackfriars. The one time I turned around, I saw the two coppers circling back to roust him."

London gave a quick nod of his head. "There you have it."

"The world is full of paranoiac individuals," I observed coolly. "Not a few of them believe that every important death—suspicious or not—is related to some single force that rules the world. Anyone with an ounce of intelligence would never take such beliefs seriously. You say you're a writer; and despite your ragged clothes, you look like a sensible enough fellow. I'm surprised you could be taken in by such a—a fairy tale."

Jack London shrugged his shoulders. Mites of dust flaked off his jacket.

"What can I say, Doctor? The old man sounded legit. I've already told you that I reported the story to Scotland Yard. But let me tell you something else. Walking around with all this information in my head makes me nervous; and, generally speaking, I'm not the nervous type. I'm not easily frightened. But I can't stop wondering about who could be next—that is, if such a tale happens to be true. The old man might be finished, but the Assassination Bureau—if it really exists—is not. Why, the geezer rambled on about hearing threats to—"

"Stop!" I cried, cutting him off. "This is crazy."

"You *too*, Doctor? And here I thought that with the police not caring, Sherlock Holmes might be able to track down the truth. I'm done now. All I can hope is that you relay the story of the Assassination Bureau to Mr Holmes. But, hey, if the ruling classes aren't interested in protecting their own, who am *I* to take up the battle?"

The ruling classes again! But, of course, what other terminology might one expect from a dedicated Socialist?

"Do you know," Jack London droned on, "that your statesmen are fond of saying, 'Wake up, England'? What they should be saying is, 'Feed up, England!'"

Enough! I wasn't going to listen to some delusional American tell me how we should run our country.

"Thank you, Mr London," said I, rising to my feet. "I've heard more than I need from you. Good day."

Jack London stood up to face me. Plopping his flat cap atop his head, he eyed me from under the short brim.

"Tell Mr Holmes hello from Johnny Upright," said he and then made for the door. Suddenly, he stopped and turned round.

"Assassination Bureau or not, Doctor, after what I've seen in East London, we might as well go back to howling savagery if this is the best that civilization can do for its people." With that parting shot, he exited the sitting room. I counted the seventeen steps he hit on his way down to the outer door.

*****

Later that evening, I met Sherlock Holmes in Simpson's at the hour named. The sky remained washed in light, and it felt strange to be wearing a heavy coat in the summer. Yet it was chillier now than it had been earlier in what already had been a cool day. Holmes was sitting at a small round table by a window that overlooked the Strand. A pair of full sherry glasses stood at the ready.

"Ah, Watson," he greeted me as I slipped off my coat. "Let me tell you of my meeting with Shinwell Johnson. I do believe that our plans regarding Baron Gruner—"

"In a moment, Holmes," said I, quickly taking my seat. "First, allow me tell you about the caller you missed this afternoon. Believe me, it won't take long. Then I shall be prepared to give my full attention to Mr Shinwell Johnson."

His face betrayed no impatience, but I could tell from the gleam in his eye that he had much to report about the case Sir James had brought to him. Still, Holmes bided his time and told me to proceed.

As quickly as I could, I furnished my account of how I had spent the hours at Baker Street listening to Jack London's tale of the Assassination Bureau. At the conclusion of my report, Holmes flashed a smile. It made him look both cynical and humorous at the same time.

"A generations-old secret organisation devoted to eliminating the people it finds objectionable? Hah, Watson, it is the Holy Grail for conspiratorial minds. How simple it would be to blame all our troubles on a single group. One need only eliminate the assemblage and—*voilà*—the problems of the world vanish."

"Listening to this Jack London, I felt much as you do—not to mention all his prattle about the ruling classes and their victims."

Sherlock Holmes sampled his sherry. "Which of the Yarders did you say called him a 'conspiracy nutter'?" he asked, cocking an eye.

"Lestrade."

Holmes snorted his approval. "Of course, it would be Lestrade. It's not often that I agree with the man," said he, raising his glass in the policeman's honour, "but in this case I shall make an exception. "A 'conspiracy nutter'," repeated Holmes with a broad smile.

His smile turned into a chortle, and then we both burst into the hearty laughter to which I referred at the start of this narrative. Only after the two of us had exhausted our mirth did we finish our sherry.

"Now, Watson," said Holmes, replacing his glass on the table, "we have the murderous machinations of Baron Gruner to discuss. His nefarious story—along with a cut of roast beef from one of those silver-domed trollies—ought to be just the thing to put Mr Jack London out of mind."

Chapter Three

Too much is written by the men who can't write
about the men who do write.
--Jack London
Martin Eden

Thanks in great part to the directions our individual lives were taking us, Sherlock Holmes and I managed to keep Jack London out of mind for much of the next eight years inclusive. As readers may remember, during that period Holmes retired to his cottage in Sussex, eventually to be joined by Mrs Hudson in her new role as housekeeper. For my part, I remarried and took a house with my new bride in Queen Anne Street. Periodically, a consultation with Scotland Yard officials might call Holmes out of retirement and back to London, but during those years we generally saw each other only on my rare visits to Sussex.

In spite of the numerous distractions, however, one could not avoid hearing of Jack London's literary achievements. After all, novels like *The Call of the Wild, The Sea Wolf, White Fang, The Iron Heel,* and *Martin Eden* helped the man create quite a name for himself in the world of *belles lettres;* and truth be told, many of our reunions did indeed find Holmes and me commenting on the success of London's latest publication.

I for one particularly enjoyed his story titled "The Scarlet Plague." Its depiction of an epidemic that decimates much of the earth's population put me in mind of Bertie Wells' tale of a world destroyed by invaders from Mars. And yet London's vivid imagination regarding relentless death also served to remind me of his belief in the phantom-like Assassination Bureau. However much I might like his fictional offerings, his apparent faith in those political murders made it exceedingly difficult to take seriously his popular writings, let alone his ever-evolving socialist philosophy.

With the low regard I held for Jack London as well as his foolish notions, one can scarcely imagine how shocked I was years later to receive a letter addressed to Holmes and me from the man himself. Like all the post sent to our former Baker Street address, the envelope had been forwarded to my literary agent, Sir Arthur Conan Doyle, who then passed it along to me. Though the letter was dated 7 May 1910, the day after His Majesty, Edward VII, had died, I didn't actually receive the missive until early July, fully two months later. It was, in fact, the death of the King that had prompted London to write.

There is no better way to convey the contents of the four-page, typed epistle than by reproducing it in its entirety. Here is the letter Jack London sent us:

Glen Ellen, Calif.
May 7, 1910.

Mr. Holmes and Dr. Watson: --

    Call me foolish, but I think this is a matter of <u>life and death.</u> I couldn't live with myself if I didn't let you know about the real danger I believe is confronting a number of important people in the world. I've got a lot of other things to attend to right now--I'm in the midst of buying up more properties than I can afford in order to create the home I've been dreaming of for as long as I can remember. But as soon as I heard about the death of your King, I decided that I had to express my fears to you.

    In retrospect, Dr Watson, I may not have been on my best behavior when we met back in 1902. I realize it's a little late for an apology, and yet I'm offering you one. Don't get me wrong. I'm not apologising for the content of my speech, only for my rudeness. I know full well that you never believed in the Assassination Bureau that I told you about all those years ago. In fact, I imagine that once you shared my story with Sherlock Holmes, the two of you probably had quite a chuckle at my expense!

Still, writer that I am, I found myself strangely fascinated by the concept of the Bureau. Even if such a murderous syndicate didn't actually exist, I thought the mere suggestion of such an outrageous gang possessed a macabre appeal, a twisted allure that readers might be attracted to-- which is why, as you may have heard, I recently decided to compose a suspense novel about that very organization. If nothing else, publishing such a story seemed like an excellent way to earn more money, which right now I am very much in need of. I was even naive enough to title the thing, "The Assassination Bureau, Ltd." The more fool I.

If you've read anything at all about the novel, I assume it's the canard going around that I bought the idea from novelist Sinclair Lewis. "Hal" (as his friends call him) is quite adept at inventing and selling miscellaneous story-lines, and it is true that last March I did in fact pay him $70 for fourteen plots. Let me assure you, however, that a story about the Assassination Bureau was not among them. No--full credit for the dangerous decision to write about the group falls entirely upon me.

In light of my current fears about that decision, however, I've been more than happy to let fester the false rumor about Lewis and the origin of the plot. Disassociating myself from the real history of the Assassination Bureau is a way to hedge my bets. That way, assuming the syndicate actually does exist, its members might not think I'm on to them. Since everybody knows that Hal keeps a trunkful of notes and newspaper stories around, I'm hoping they'll think that he concocted an outline from some account he'd read in the public press and then simply sold it to me.

Remember the old man, the self-confessed assassin, from whom I first learned about the Bureau? Trust that I too was skeptical when he told me of its devilish intent. Yet now I have reason to take things more seriously. I don't know if you recall, Doctor, but I haven't forgotten that you cut me off in mid-speech before I could tell you the names of the additional people I had heard were targets, and it's bothered me ever since. If you hadn't stopped me, you would have learned that foremost among the intended targets was your King.

I tell you now that the old man at the Salvation Army barracks said the Bureau not only had Edward in its crosshairs, but also had plans for staging his murder so that it would look like a natural death--and that's exactly what happened. In fact, I just read that Sir James Reid, the Royal Doctor, announced that Edward died from a series of heart attacks. Remember the germs, Doctor? They can fool the best of medical minds.

Another person mentioned by the old man that day was killed a while ago--"Soapy" Smith--though neither of you would have reason to know of him. A number of years back, he was the crime boss of Denver, Colorado, here in the States. I only remember his name since he ended up in Alaska at the same time I was in the Klondike. But even as far north as I'd gone, there were rumors about the infamous gunfight on the Juneau Wharf in Skaguay.

The shoot-out took place in 1898, and that's where they killed him. A vigilante group called the Committee of 101 shot Smith dead, and almost immediately people were saying that outsiders had infiltrated the Committee. What's more, one of the vigilantes was named Frank Reid. Whether or not he was related to King Edward's Dr. Reid, it's not too far a stretch to figure that the outsiders who penetrated the Committee were agents of the Assassination Bureau.

I'm one who believes it anyhow. In fact, King Edward's death has convinced me more than ever that the Assassination Bureau is real. And once I started thinking that the deaths predicted by the old man might be more than coincidence, I began to worry. The syndicate may work slowly, gentlemen, but its results are deadly. That's why I'm so concerned.

You see, there were four other names the old man mentioned as targets who (at least, so far) remain among the living--here in America, our former President, Theodore Roosevelt, and the famous journalist, David Graham Phillips; in London, a banker named Charles Morton-Watt; and one Mycroft Holmes, who the old man said had connections to the British government. From reading Dr. Watson's accounts, Mr. Holmes, I know this Mycroft is your brother; and as soon as I heard about the death of your King, I reckoned I shouldn't be wasting any more time in alerting you.

It's personal on my side as well. I've actually met David Graham Phillips. He was introduced to me a few years ago in New York by Bailey Millard, the editor of Cosmopolitan. Bailey thought Phillips and I would get along since we shared so many of the same political views, but then we didn't hit it off. Phillips is too high-toned for my taste, and I don't think he cared much for my working-class clothes—my flannel shirt and dungarees. (I didn't even wear a waistcoat, and it was the middle of winter!) I was pretty annoyed by the whole business though Bailey thought I'd done Phillips an injustice. In the long run, I suppose Bailey knows what he's talking about. After all, Phillips stays on the right side of the issues, and there are so few of us with socialistic leanings that we really can't afford to bicker.

How the two of you respond to all this news is your business, but I can tell you right now that I'm planning to lie low. Even though I've written two-thirds of The Assassination Bureau, Ltd., I'm putting it aside. For all I care, somebody else can finish it. The murder of Soapy Smith may not have convinced me, but the death of King Edward most certainly has--it's not safe or healthy to admit knowing anything about such a group of killers, let alone write a book about them.

Make what you want to of these comments, gentlemen. I've been burned once by talking to the police, and I've got my own headaches out here in California trying to create a corner of paradise for my wife and me. As I recall saying once before, at least all the worry about the Assassination Bureau is finally off my back.

Sincerely,

Jack London

Two of the so-called targets mentioned by London were personally familiar to us. Holmes' connection to his brother Mycroft was obvious. (I might add that, however morbid, seeing Mycroft's name included on a list with a former President of the United States and the late King of England corroborated the importance I have always bestowed upon the man.)

As for David Graham Phillips, Holmes and I had met the pressman back in the middle 90's when he had come by Baker Street to thank Holmes for helping him with a news story. Touring the Levant in '93 shortly after his supposed death at the hands of Moriarty, Holmes had managed to get the news of a British naval disaster to Phillips who was then in London. More to the point, Phillips had gained fame in his own country for writing a series of articles accusing the American Senate of treason. No doubt, he had angered a number of important people.

Of the remaining two figures London had mentioned, Theodore Roosevelt was world-famous, well known for his political, military, and peripatetic adventures. The name of Charles Morton-Watt, on the other hand, hovered in the ether as a result of malicious rumour.

A young banker during the Second Boer War, Morton-Watt had supposedly made a lot of money by embezzling funds set aside for weapons. Naïve investors thought they were supporting the British army whilst Morgan-Watt—or so the story runs—diverted the money into guns that ultimately came to be used against our own soldiers.

To separate people from their savings, Morgan-Watt was alleged to have avoided rich investors, appealing instead to the patriotism of the less-sophisticated commoners. Although such treasonous acts were never proved, additional tales of underhanded financial transactions continued to plague him.

It must be remembered, of course, that regurgitating the names of people purportedly threatened with murder confirmed nothing. In spite of Jack London's newly-formed certainty regarding the Assassination Bureau, the repetition of a list of possible targets recalled by a delusional old man in no way furnished proof as to the existence of the organisation. Nor did claiming that King Edward had been murdered make such a crime any more real. At the very least however, the wild charges encompassed a possible threat to Mycroft Holmes; and as a result I felt compelled by loyalty to convey them to his brother.

No sooner did I finish reading London's letter, therefore, than I wired Holmes of my intention to call upon him; and the following day, I whirled down to Sussex aboard the morning train. After securing the proper connections in Eastbourne and Fulworth, I ultimately found myself at Holmes' cottage by the sea.

*****

"Oh, Dr Watson," Mrs Hudson greeted me upon my arrival, "how wonderful it is to see you. You must come down more often."

"Thank you, Mrs Hudson," said I. "It's always a pleasure."

Our former landlady asked after my wife; but she could also observe that at the same time I was answering, I was also searching for my old friend amidst the familiar clutter—the stacks of books, the piles of newspaper cuttings, the used test tubes.

Undaunted, she smoothed down her white apron and waved in the direction of a neatly set table. "You're just in time for luncheon," said she, "but we'll have to wait for Mr Holmes. He's currently upstairs ridding himself of his beekeeper's costume. He's been out among his hives all morning."

Within minutes, my friend appeared in his favourite mouse-coloured dressing gown; and following a perfunctory exchange of greetings, we sat down at table. Hardly had we settled into our chairs when Mrs Hudson placed before each of us a bowl of steaming tomato bisque.

"Now, Watson," said Holmes, rubbing his hands together, "pray, tell me what is so urgent that it requires our immediate discussion."

I could not tell if Holmes' enthusiasm was based on his desire to hear my news or to sample Mrs Hudson's soup. But when I produced Jack London's letter from inside my coat pocket, Holmes put down his spoon and took up the missive.

"Ah hah!" said he after scanning the first few paragraphs, "I see that even after eight years, the fear monger is still at his job." In spite of such disdain, however, he continued to read.

For my part, I couldn't help noting a worried Mrs Hudson looking in from the kitchen. Preoccupied with Jack London's jeremiad, Holmes was prolonging the soup course; and her furrowed brow suggested that she feared overcooking her *entrée.*

"Bleat!" Holmes ejaculated upon completing the epistle. "Utter bleat!" Tossing the pages on the table, he proceeded to accommodate his housekeeper by consuming the bisque.

Immediately thereafter, Mrs Hudson placed before us an aromatic platter of fillet of sole; and Holmes and I delayed our debate until we had served ourselves.

"Surely, Watson," said Holmes between bites, "you don't expect me to approach my brother with the contents expressed in this letter. Such speculation was silly in 1902, and it is equally silly today. Mycroft will laugh me out of Whitehall if I come to him with toothless threats aimed at distinguished Americans like Theodore Roosevelt and David Graham Phillips, let alone himself. These are warnings based on flimsy rumour and silly coincidence. No, Watson, assuming I actually did want to convince my brother that some preposterous organisation was planning to kill him, I would need to be in possession of hard-boiled *facts*."

I was put in mind of Dickens' Mr Gradgrind. "Fact, fact, fact!" the pedagogue would demand though I doubted Sherlock Holmes had ever heard of him.

"*Proof!*" Holmes went on. "How else to verify the reality of this so-called Assassination Bureau? An agency, I should add, that I myself do not believe exists. Without *facts*, Mycroft—as well as any others on the purported list—would face needless concern and worry. I'm sorry for your trouble, old fellow, though I do appreciate your taking the train down from London."

Knowing Holmes' practical nature as I did, I could not have expected him to react in any other way. But because the threat, real or otherwise, involved his brother, it would have been churlish for me not to have informed him of Jack London's paranoia. If Mycroft Holmes was not to be told of the alleged threat, let that decision be made by a relation and not by me. I failed to regard my mission as a complete loss, however. At the very least, it had garnered for me one of Mrs Hudson's coveted meals.

Chapter Four

From emperor and king down to the humblest peasant—
we accept them all, if—and it is a big if—
if their execution is decided to be socially justifiable.
--Jack London
The Assassination Bureau, Ltd.

Though I did not recognise it at the time, my belief in the Assassination Bureau began to solidify on 25 January 1911. That was the day I read in the *Times* of the murder of David Graham Phillips. The poor man had been shot in New York's Gramercy Park on the 23rd and had died the day after. I had met him just that one day in Baker Street, but needless to say, I was shocked and mourned the loss of a gifted acquaintance.

Still, with no evidence to connect Phillips' death to the prediction of his murder in the letter Jack London had sent us more than half a year before, I paid scant attention to the details of the matter. As I wrote to Holmes, the newspaper reported the shooting to have been the singular act of a madman.

And yet neither Holmes nor I could escape involvement. Phillips' sister, Mrs Carolyn Frevert, knew of Graham's visit to Baker Street; and in March of 1912, just under two months following the one-year anniversary of her brother's death, she came to England with the purpose of prompting Holmes to investigate some curiosities in the official report of the shooting. For details regarding the success of her quest and our subsequent journey to New York, one may consult my own account of the case, which I titled *The Seventh Bullet*.

In spite of the accuracy of my narrative, it still needs to be said that I did withhold some minor facts that at the time I considered irrelevant to our investigation. Though Phillips' political writings had clearly antagonised many in the upper classes, Holmes and I could find no links between his murder and any widespread international syndicate like the Assassination Bureau. Consequently, I omitted from *The Seventh Bullet* any reports of my meetings with Holmes in the fall of 1912 related to our evolving sense of some worldwide conspiracy.

Infrequent as such meetings were, recording them would have created the false impression that Holmes and I were involved in some sort of active investigation. In truth, Holmes and I seldom worked together following his retirement. Indeed, after returning from New York, Sherlock Holmes seemed quite content to reacquaint himself with his bee colonies in the Sussex Downs.

I, however, maintained no such responsibilities; and it was not long after Holmes' departure from London that I gained an important insight. Having been exposed to the vagaries of the criminal mind through our work together, I found myself hungering to learn more. Detecting, I discovered, had caught my fancy; and with no Sherlock Holmes in the vicinity, I began to cultivate my own professional relationship with Scotland Yard.

On not a few occasions, I was pleased to contribute my medical expertise (such as it was) to investigations conducted by the Metropolitan Police. In point of fact, my work for the Yard went on for years following Holmes' retirement; and as a result, I, unlike most common citizens, was never particularly surprised to discover uniformed constables at my door. My wife was the one who never grew accustomed to their presence.

It was just such a visitation from the police that re-enforced my certainty in the existence of the Assassination Bureau. The event in question occurred late one dark, rainy afternoon towards the end of April in 1912. The general melancholy associated with the sinking of the *Titanic* still hovered in the air, and the downpour had done nothing to wash it away.

Our housekeeper answered the clang of the bell.

"Is this the home of Dr John Watson?" I heard a clipped male voice ask above the steady tattoo of raindrops.

"That's all right, Mrs Meeks," said I, hurrying towards the open door. I knew that whoever was out there stood only partially sheltered beneath our small porch roof, and I wanted to usher the person out of the rain as quickly as possible. It turned out to be a uniformed policeman draped in a shiny black slicker. I welcomed him into the entrance hall and identified myself.

"Sir," said he, the water from his slicker dripping onto our vestibule carpet, "Inspector MacKinnon has asked if you could accompany me to the Old Bell Tavern in Fleet Street."

"MacKinnon," I repeated, picturing the Inspector's grand walrus-moustache. We'd first worked together more than ten years before on the Amberley case, an investigation that I reported much later in the sketch called "The Retired Colourman". Concerned that Holmes would be the one to solve the problem (as indeed he had), MacKinnon turned quite appreciative of my friend when Holmes allowed the credit to be given to the Inspector. As a result, the two had got along ever since.

"Has there been a crime?" I asked.

"A murder, sir."

"A murder is it?" I raised my eyebrows. "Let me get my things. I'll join you in a moment."

"I'll wait for you in the motor just outside," said he and, informally saluting me, exited into the rain.

Though I no longer maintained an active surgery in 1912, I did make myself available for the occasional consultation with former patients. Fortunately, on this day there was no one scheduled. Thus, I donned my waterproof and, grabbing my medical bag, bowler, and umbrella, informed my wife that I was to be engaged with work that afternoon for Scotland Yard.

Glistening in the rain, the black police motorcar stood growling at the end of our stone path. I opened my brolly and through the downpour negotiated my way along the drenched flags until I landed safely on the unforgiving cushions inside the car. The machine lurched forward, and almost immediately the sweeps of the windscreen wipers provided metronymic accompaniment to our drive. The bright lights and oncoming headlamps reflected in the soggy roadway as we rumbled along Queen Anne Street; and soon after joining the tangle of London traffic on Southampton Row, we were motoring southeast down the Strand.

The Old Bell Tavern in Fleet Street is among the oldest public houses in London. Designed by Sir Christopher Wren in the early-seventeenth century, it was intended for the convenience of the stonemasons constructing St. Paul's. Today, despite the sheets of rain, the bright light, which shone through the Tavern's half-curtained windows, made the establishment clearly noticeable. We rolled to a halt directly before the entrance.

Disdaining the need to open my umbrella, I made the short dash to the door and quickly found myself inside, trickling water onto the small stone floor at the entrance. To my left and right stood a pair of wooden tables, and a few feet beyond rose a handsome bar of polished dark wood. The taproom looked ready for business, but there were no patrons within; the tavern was closed.

It was not empty, however. At a wooden table at the centre of the illuminated tableau sat the bloodied body of a grey-haired man dressed in a dark, well-tailored suit. Slumped forward, he sat with his disfigured head face down on the red-splattered table top amidst the plates and tankards before him. A pool of blood had spread beneath his chest, the crimson liquid having worked its way to the edge of the table and dribbled onto the floor where it had formed an additional but smaller puddle near his patent-leather boots. Needless to say, the man appeared quite dead.

Yet strangely, it wasn't the body that surprised me the most at this ghastly scene. It was the presence of Mr Sherlock Holmes. As far as I knew, he had planned to stay put with his bees in Sussex following the resolution of the Phillips affair.

"*Holmes!*" I managed to blurt out.

"Ah, friend Watson," said he, "good of you to come." He was dressed in his traditional inverness cape and ear-flapped traveling cap.

"Good afternoon, Doctor," Inspector MacKinnon greeted me, removing his bowler in the process. "Sorry to bring you out on a day like this, but murder has no call to wait for good weather, you know." He spoke with a lilting inflection quite out of place for so morbid a scene.

"Good afternoon, gentlemen," I replied, hoping my professionalism might mask my confusion. "What's happened here?"

"Bloke was shot twice," the policeman answered matter-of-factly. "Once in the head; once in the chest. We have the man who did it—a fellow called Wainwright—as well as the pocket-gun he did it with."

"Good work," said I.

"Thank you, Doctor. It's really quite cut and dried. The killer came in, shouted something at the victim about losing his life savings, and fired at him twice. Still, I know how you and Mr Holmes like to be consulted on these dramatic cases, and I feel certain that this case will be in all the papers."

"Quite right, MacKinnon," said my friend, "given the identity of the deceased. It's why I made the journey up from Sussex."

"Why call it a 'dramatic case'?" I asked. "Who is the poor wretch?"

Sherlock Holmes flashed one of his amused but cynical smiles. "I hesitate to tell you, old fellow. It is a name with which you are familiar. The murdered man is none other than Mr Charles Morton-Watt, the infamous financial wizard."

Charles Morton-Watt! A thrill of horror coursed through me when I heard the name. It had been almost a year since London's letter had identified the dead man before us as another prospective target of the Assassination Bureau, but clearly I had not forgot the warning. Obviously, neither had Holmes.

Suddenly, it dawned upon me. Though I may have successfully fooled myself into ignoring Jack London's paranoiac aspersions for a while, I could no longer conceal my suspicions. Thoughts of an insidious and far-reaching conspiracy, I was now forced to admit, had been lingering in the back of my mind ever since January when I had first heard of the murder of David Graham Phillips.

"He enjoyed mingling with the common folk," observed the Inspector. "People said that's what he was doing here."

For the moment, however, I was envisioning a broader picture than the scene in the Old Bell Tavern. If a banker could be murdered in so populous a place as a public house and David Graham Phillips could be shot down on a sidewalk in the middle of New York City, did it not follow that—however preposterous the concept appeared—attempts on the life of Theodore Roosevelt and Mycroft Holmes might be imminent? Perhaps, it was finally time for attention to be paid.

Listen to me, I thought to myself, *I'm starting to sound like Jack London.*

"Do you wish to examine the body then, Doctor?" MacKinnon asked.

Lost in my conspiratorial hypotheses, I nodded numbly and laid my hat, coat, and umbrella on a nearby chair.

"If you don't mind," said Holmes to the Inspector, "I'll conduct my own investigations."

The policeman encompassed the entire taproom with a wave of his bowler. "You go right ahead, Mr Holmes," he laughed. "Look anywhere you wish. All I know is that we've caught the villain red-handed. Somebody grabbed him while he still held his smoking Derringer. He'd fired both barrels—twenty-two calibre bullets."

Like a gunfighter from the American West, the heavily-moustached MacKinnon struck a pose opposite the dead man, his right arm extending straight out, the hand held gun-like—thumb up, index finger pointed directly at the corpse. Emphasising the recoil, he jerked his arm each time he barked news of the shot: "*Bang!* One bullet struck him in the head. *Bang!* The second bullet hit him in the chest. Case closed."

I made my way among the chairs to what was left of Charles Morton-Watt. Strangely, or so I thought at the time, Holmes moved off in the opposite direction, manoeuvring past a pair of tables to reach the front windows. Drawing the white curtains aside, he took a brief look at the panes down which, like falling tears, coursed countless rivulets of rain. Almost immediately, however, he concentrated his examination on the woodwork that framed the glass. MacKinnon scratched his head, a classic portrait of confusion.

Meanwhile, I looked at the dead man. At first glance, the Inspector seemed correct. Buckled over the table as the body was, it was easy to see both the exit wound in the back from the bullet hole in the chest and the severe damage to the occipital bone at the rear of the skull caused by the bullet to the forehead. It all seemed clear enough. And yet I could sense that something was wrong.

The Derringer is a small-calibre weapon, and both the bullet hole to the forehead and the resulting cavity at the rear seemed much too large for single shots. What's more, a careful inspection of the bullet hole in the back of Morton-Watt's bloodied jacket revealed the unmistakeable burn-marks from a pistol fired at close range. That the hole itself was too neat for an exit wound became redundant in light of the powder-blackening on the fabric.

At the same time I made these discoveries, Holmes was employing his magnifying glass to scrutinise the right side of the wooden window frame.

Shortly, I heard him utter a cry of satisfaction; but when I turned to face him, his expression remained stoical, his eye still close to the lens.

"Holmes?" I queried.

He looked at me with a quick glance. "Well, Watson," he asked, "what do you make of it?"

"Two points jump out." As I spoke, I noted Inspector MacKinnon's smile, hooded as it was by his moustache, slowly disappear. "There is altogether too much destruction at the back of the skull to be the result of a single twenty-two-calibre bullet to the head. I suspect it would have required at least two such missiles to create this kind of mess. Assuming I am correct, further examination should reveal that the large entry hole in the forehead is in actuality the identical spot where two bullets entered the skull, one immediately after the other. What's more, the powder burns at the back of the coat indicate the poor man was also shot from behind."

"Excellent, Watson!" cried Holmes. "I shall make a detective of you yet!"

I always enjoyed Holmes' compliments—in spite of the smudge of sarcasm that so frequently accompanied them. Inspector MacKinnon, however, was not so pleased.

"A pair of shots to the head and one in the back require more than Mr Wainwright's two-bullet Derringer," said he, shaking his head. "Three shots mean a second shooter. Witnesses—and there were plenty of them—reported hearing only the two."

"My dear MacKinnon," observed Holmes matter-of-factly, "the shot in the back occurred at precisely the same moment as one of the head-shots. That would account for people saying they'd heard only two reports."

"Mere theory, Mr Holmes," said the Inspector. "A barmaid standing just behind the victim was quite insistent that she'd heard only the two shots. She repeated herself a few times to make sure we'd taken her statement correctly. And I've already told you, we've got our man—John Wainwright, a disgruntled investor in one of Morton-Watt's shady business schemes."

"And yet," said I, my confidence strengthened by Holmes' support, "I'm certain that a police autopsy will verify my conclusions."

MacKinnon, now holding his bowler behind him with both hands, rocked slowly back and forth. He appeared uninterested in my findings.

"Gentlemen," said the policeman, "I repeat: we already have our man. I didn't invite the two of you here to open a new can of worms."

Sherlock Holmes offered the Inspector a beguiling smile. "Come, Watson. It is obvious our services are no longer needed."

I collected my coat and umbrella and, tipping my hat to MacKinnon, followed Holmes out into the darkness. The rain had subsided to a gentle drizzle, but I opened the brolly anyway.

Holmes was content to let his inverness protect him as we began walking up Fleet Street in the direction of the Strand.

After a few paces, however, he leaned in under my umbrella in order to be heard. "You're quite right," said he. "The man was doubtlessly struck twice in the head by the two bullets from Wainwright's Derringer and—at precisely the same moment—shot through the back with a much more powerful pistol by someone standing behind him. Having made up their minds, the police didn't bother to look."

"But in the name of Justice—"

"As you know, old fellow, it's especially comforting for the Yarders to ignore loose ends in closing up these sensational crimes. They like to put such cases to bed. But I discovered a bullet lodged in the woodwork, the bullet that had been fired into Morton-Watt's back. It passed straight through the body and proves that a second shooter had fired at Morton-Watt from the rear. It's fortunate no one else was hit during its flight."

"But who could have done such a dreadful deed?"

"Quite possibly, the very barmaid who insisted so vocally on having heard only two shots. MacKinnon said she was directly behind the victim."

"A female shooter, Holmes?"

"And why not? Though it is the era of the New Woman, I imagine suspicion would be less likely to fall upon a female executioner."

"Executioner?"

"Oh, yes. Make no mistake about it. This Charles Morton-Watt wasn't just *killed* last night. He was executed."

I paused for a moment to allow this observation to sink in. It flitted about with my own suspicions regarding the Assassination Bureau, suspicions I had so far hesitated to resurrect aloud. Instead, I remained practical.

"But even if it *was* a woman who committed the crime," I ventured, "how could a second shooter go undetected? MacKinnon said the pub was crowded."

"Classic diversion, Watson. Wainwright was shouting and waving his Derringer about. Everyone was looking at *him*. No doubt the second gun was concealed—perhaps in a towel carried by the barmaid—if not by someone else. The second shooter's job was to fire at precisely the same moment Wainwright did. It's of no consequence now, however. Were one to investigate more fully, I'm certain he would discover that, no matter the identity of the second shooter, he—or she—has long since disappeared."

We stopped beneath an electric street lamp in order to be more easily seen by passing cabs. A veil of illuminated mist encompassed the light. "You'll stay with us tonight," said I to my companion. "Dinner's included. Our cook is quite capable of serving three. I believe rack of lamb is on the menu."

"Thank you, old fellow," said Holmes, rubbing his hands together as I hailed a taxi. "Your invitation sounds much more appealing than a late train back to Sussex."

I must confess that my offer was not purely altruistic. First, Phillips; now Morton-Watt. It was time to discuss my fears about the Assassination Bureau with Holmes. No longer could any reasonable person who had read Jack London's letter ignore the implications of a second shooter in the Bell Tavern. To me, the mysterious second assassin that Holmes envisioned at the murder scene seemed not unlike those unknown vigilantes on Juneau Wharf, the self-styled executioners who, as described by London, had shot and killed "Soapy" Smith in the name of preserving law and order.

With additional shooters on hand to make certain the "job" was done right, the murders of Smith in Alaska and now Morton-Watt in the Old Bell Tavern seemed anything but simple. Though vaguely disguised as revenge-killings, I believed that one would be hard-pressed not to call them what they really were— "assassinations".

It made complete sense to me, and in the taxi I offered my interpretation to Holmes.

"Coincidence," he snapped.

"I thought detectives don't believe in coincidences."

"As a general rule, Watson, that is the case. But have you forgot the investigation of the man called Black Peter, which you yourself recorded? Though the initials, 'P.C.', were found on the sealskin tobacco-pouch in Black Peter's cabin, they turned out to belong not to Peter Carey but to Patrick Cairns. Had friend Hopkins recognised the simple coincidence in the matter, he himself might have cornered the true murderer."

"But surely, Holmes, that was different. It was but a minor point in a single crime. In this case we're discussing a series of murders with multiple similarities. In such instances, dismissing the presence of coincidences could be fatal."

"Perhaps—but one must be careful. It is the seductive nature of coincidence, old fellow, that enables visionaries to concoct the most fantastical of conspiracy theories. What's next? Are you going to tell me that the Assassination Bureau miraculously conspired to run the *Titanic* into an iceberg? How many times must I say it? The Assassination Bureau is a fiction, Watson. For me to believe in it, you'll have to produce the evidence that proves its existence; and, mind you, I don't think you'll be getting any help to do so from your friends at Scotland Yard."

His remonstrance to the contrary, I refused to be put off. "I take it, then," said I defiantly, "that you still won't warn your brother."

"*He* will tell you the same thing I just did, old fellow: without sound facts to prove it, no conspiracy exists."

So ended our discussion—but not my own newfound certainty. I remained fully convinced that there was more to these murders than Holmes was willing to admit. A quiet tension hovered over our dinner that evening. Breakfast the next morning was similar. In the end, I offered Holmes a grim farewell as he secured a taxi for Victoria and effected his return to Sussex. By that time, at least, the rain had ended.

Chapter Five

It is the king of words—Power.
Not God, not Mammon, but Power.
Pour it over your tongue till it tingles with it.
Power.
--Jack London
The Iron Heel

Sherlock Holmes may not have been stirred into action by the murder of Charles Morton-Watt, but I was. At the very least, someone had to protect Brother Mycroft.

Like Holmes, I too tended not to believe in coincidences— at least, not those that trivialised questions of life and death. But regarding the Assassination Bureau, I now perceived too many connections among a number of murders—both past and predicted—to ignore. Holmes would consider me paranoiac; but given the possible attacks on human lives that I might be able to prevent, his was a condemnation I was willing to suffer.

Besides, there was also the Coroner's report from the Morton-Watt autopsy. Inspector Mackinnon had sent me the results, which substantiated my view of the affair: three shots, two shooters. Confirmation that Wainwright had a confederate may not have proved to Sherlock Holmes the existence of an international conspiracy, but the official findings were enough for me.

It was time to take some sort of action. In spite of Holmes' scepticism, I vowed to do my utmost to protect those who had been threatened. However high-minded the leaders of the Assassination Bureau might consider themselves, no independent organisation could be allowed to wield the power of life or death with impunity. Though Holmes and the police showed little interest, I would do whatever I could to uncover evidence of their nefarious plots.

To that end, I constructed a plan. First, I would locate Shinwell Johnson, Holmes' one-time informant, whose criminal history allowed him access to London's underworld—the same Shinwell Johnson I've already mentioned in connection with helping Holmes solve the case of "The Illustrious Client" many years before. Johnson could be counted on, I knew, as long as it was understood that he remain in the background. To reveal his true role in the criminal conviction of a wrongdoer would place his life in danger.

"Stand me up to testify at the Old Bailey," said he on a visit to Baker Street, "and that's the end of Porky Shinwell."

Not that the man had any inhibitions about being seen in public. On the contrary, I remembered that he had a favourite table in the Northumberland Arms, a public house on Northumberland Street.

"The Northumberland's easy to find," he had told Holmes and me one day in Baker Street.

It goes without saying that both of us were well acquainted with the territory. The pub stands adjacent to the narrow walkway called Craven Passage, which lies between the Northumberland and Nevill's, the Turkish baths where Holmes and I had discussed the meeting with Sir James Damery on the day I first met Jack London. Faithful readers may also recall that it was in the hotel above the Northumberland that Sir Henry Baskerville discovered his boots had been stolen.

In spite of our familiarity with the area, the informant added with an ironical note that I am sure was unintended, "The Northumberland's close enough to Scotland Yard to spit on."

Suffice it to say, that on the trail of Shinwell Johnson I journeyed by cab to Northumberland Street one silent, moonless night in late spring. Nearby, the tower of Westminster rose up, a large black mass save for the round, electrically-lit face of the clock. The hands showed 9.00 whilst Big Ben, the great bell housed within the tower, sounded its chimes in confirmation. Once the final tones died away, all was quiet again.

No sooner did I enter the Northumberland Arms, however, than a cacophony of loud voices and raucous laughter crashed over me; and it was through a tangle of red and sweaty faces, waving arms, and hoisted tankards that I was forced to scan for the visage belonging to Johnson. Yet I could not spot my prey and had to enquire of a young barmaid for the man.

Now it has always interested me that women can exude a kind of fetching beauty when they are in the midst of hard work, and attraction must be farthest from their minds. So it was with this barmaid. The night might have been chilly, but a patina of perspiration shone on her forehead, and a thin line of moisture appeared just above her upper lip. Still, her bouncing ringlets of raven-black hair, parted wet lips of ruby-red, and low-scooped white blouse exposing an ample swell of *décolletage* made this old man's heart race. But I digress.

"Shinwell Johnson," she parroted with a decided cockney lilt. Then she broke into a grin and gave me a little poke. "Oh, luv, you mean *Porky* Shinwell."

"P-Porky," I stammered, "the very one."

"'E's at 'is table. It's in the back, innit?" And she nodded vaguely in a direction to the rear of the bar.

I elbowed my way through the boisterous patrons; but Johnson spotted me before I saw him. I was about to approach his table when he flicked his head in a manner, which I took to mean, "We'll meet outside."

Turning round, I found myself pushing back through the same crowd I had only just disrupted, facing fewer smiling faces among those whom I had already edged out of the way. But make it I did; and after exiting, I veered left into the dimly-lit passage between the pub and Nevill's.

Shinwell Johnson appeared a few minutes later, his long coat failing to conceal his growing girth, his salt-and-pepper hair askew. Clearly, even years after his work for Sherlock Holmes had ended, Johnson feared calling attention to his relationship with the "authorities"—which, I should imagine, now included me. He looked up and down the walkway; and when he spoke, his voice was almost a whisper.

"Well, well," said he, "if it ain't m' old pal, Dr Watson."

"Shinwell," I nodded

"How's our Mr Holmes doing then?" he asked.

"Fine. I'll tell him you enquired."

"So what brings *you* round? You don't often show up without him. In fact, *never.*"

"I've been asked by officials at Scotland Yard to help in the investigation of the recent shooting death of Charles Morton-Watt." I may have stretched the timing a bit, but the statement was essentially true.

"I thought the coppers already nicked somebody," said he. "A bloke named Wainwright—or so I've been told."

My cynical smirk must have betrayed Holmes' and my suspicions because Johnson immediately responded, "Oh, that's how it is, is it? More *to* the thing than just the one shooter." He paused to look round, as if for spies or eavesdroppers, and then whispered conspiratorially, "—that is, if the poor sod they've nabbed done it at all."

I refused the bait. I wouldn't reveal our misgivings. "Any word on the street about it?" I asked. Thinking of the barmaid Holmes had in mind, I added, "Anything at all, say, about a *woman* who might have participated in a shooting?"

Shinwell narrowed his dark eyes and stroked the stubble on his chin. "Well," said he, "I did hear tell of someone come down from Liverpool 'bout two months ago. Maybe a Russian. Supposed to be pretty handy with a piece. Could be it was a woman. Nobody said. Not that a woman shooter's common, mind."

"What about the gun itself?" I asked. "Anything about a pistol somebody wanted to get rid of in the last day or so?"

Shinwell Johnson let out a slow, ropey laugh that emanated from deep inside his chest. With a thumb, he gestured toward the Thames off in the darkness behind us. "Easiest way to get rid of a gun, Doctor, is to heave it in the river."

"I've always thought there was money to be made from *selling* a firearm."

"Aye," said he, "but if the police've already caught the fella they think done it and you're still saying there might be an unknown shooter on the loose, I'm thinking he—or she—is a professional and more concerned with eliminating the evidence than cashing in on the extra quid or two—if you get my meaning."

I did get his meaning. I also recalled how Holmes had phrased it in our very first case together: "Political assassins are only too glad to do their work and fly."

I gave him my card and said I would be much obliged if he let me know as quickly as possible if he heard anything about these matters.

"Aye, Doctor," said he again, his voice still low. "Don't be forgetting to give my regards to Mr Holmes." With those parting words, the big man touched his fingers to his forelock and marched back into the pub.

Now it was *my* turn to look up and down the dim, narrow walkway. I saw no one stirring. And yet it was night-time; and there were enough darkened doorways, like the ladies' entrance to Nevill's, in which some nefarious figure might have listened in on our conversation. Not that there had been anything of great import to learn. In fact, unhappy with my lack of specific results, I waved down a passing cab for the drive back to Queen Anne Street.

Though the ride itself was uneventful that dark night, a strange occurrence took place upon my return home. The cab deposited me across the road from my house, and I happened to notice that the nearest electric street lamp remained unlit. Forced to traverse the road in darkness, I heard my footfalls echoing into the gloom.

Suddenly, the roar of a motor broke the silence, and the glare of bright headlights riveted my attention. No sooner did I step onto the street than a powerful motor-car came hurtling towards me.

Bloody hell! I thought, and only by throwing myself down against the kerb did I manage to avoid the car's menacing fender. An instant later, the car had vanished.

"Blackguard!" I shouted, rising and shaking my fist in its wake.

Did someone just try to run me down? I wondered as I brushed myself off. Had some villain followed me from the Old Bell Tavern with my death in mind? Might a driver with murderous intent have been lurking down the road awaiting my appearance and then taken deliberate aim at me? Could the Assassination Bureau, I inevitably found myself asking, have known all along what I was up to and tried to put a stop to it?

Or might there have been a more innocent explanation? Perhaps the driver had been some thrill-seeker in front of whom I had the misfortune of crossing—or simply someone who had had too much to drink.

None the worse for wear, I unlocked the front door and entered the quiet house. Of only one thing was I certain. In no way would I burden my wife with even the slightest hint that an attempt on her husband's life might just have occurred outside her curtained window.

*****

Once safely within the confines of my study, I gave no more thought to my narrow escape. On the contrary, settling myself at my writing desk, I intended to put into motion the second part of the plan I hoped would put an end to the Assassination Bureau. I had already located Shinwell Johnson— though so far, at least, little good had come of it. I needed to do better. With the expectation of learning more than I had at the Northumberland Arms, I sought to make contact with another former acquaintance, Agent Leverton of the Pinkertons, the American detective agency.

I had met the man a number of years before while aiding Holmes in the pursuit of an organisation also notorious for its killings, an anarchistic gang called the Red Circle. With tentacles stretching from Europe to America, the Red Circle had prompted

Leverton's journey to England. On the trail of one Giuseppi "Black" Gorgianno, a vicious murderer with possible ties to the old Carbonari, Agent Leverton obviously had experience with the type of twisted souls who comprised the membership of groups bent on political murder. The Pinkertons, after all, had been in the business of protecting American Presidents since the time of Abraham Lincoln.

My intention was to send a cable to Leverton for information regarding the current health and welfare of another of the supposed targets to whom Jack London's letter had referred, former President Theodore Roosevelt, an unforgettable personage whom I had actually met in New York during our investigation of the Phillips shooting. I hoped that a cable to Leverton about any known groups in the States seeking to harm the "Colonel", as Roosevelt liked to call himself, might yield worthwhile information about similar organisations operating in England.

In composing the message, I wrote of my concern for Roosevelt in light of rumours I had heard, rumours about a ruthless syndicate seeking to assassinate political figures. With no way of knowing how credible such stories might be, I told him that, whilst I hoped to avoid creating a crisis, I was seeking any information along those lines that might have come his way. I didn't refer to the Assassination Bureau by name or indicate that

Roosevelt himself had been mentioned as a possible target—though I did suggest that Leverton caution the Colonel's bodyguards to remain particularly alert.

I knew the agent to be a reliable man, but I was none the less surprised by the promptness of his reply. I had sent my message the morning after my visit to the Northumberland Arms, and a uniformed messenger boy appeared at my door late that same day with the cabled response.

The reply read: "Single agent, Frank Hopkins, assigned to Roosevelt. Reports to be sent directly to you from Hopkins." In addition, Leverton wrote: "In 1903, one major incident regarding TR. Secret Service arrested man with pistol at Sagamore Hill, TR's home. Suspect planned to kill the President." That arrest may have been nine years before, but it might well have signalled the start of the Assassination Bureau's deadly campaign against the Colonel.

Now I hadn't followed American politics very closely, but I did know that Roosevelt was currently running for President in a progressive political party nicknamed "Bullmoose". Though I could not cite the details, I recalled that many of Roosevelt's criticisms seemed aimed at the business community in particular, certainly a stance destined to engender resentment.

But would the political views of a mere candidate—as the former President was now presenting himself—be sufficient to spark a murderous attack upon his person? To what end? Would not someone who wanted to eliminate Roosevelt be wiser to commit the deed only if Roosevelt were actually elected President again? Attempting the murder before the election risked unnecessary exposure. After all, most experts were predicting that the Colonel had little chance of winning (despite the support, I feel compelled to add, of William Gillette, the stage-actor celebrated for his portrayals of Sherlock Holmes).

On the other hand, such a murderous attempt might be the product of the contract begun in '03 and yet to be completed. As Jack London had written us, though the Assassination Bureau might work slowly, it could be counted on to work with certainty. One imagines that a ruthless patron would not quibble over the timing as long as the target was ultimately eliminated.

I waited anxiously through the summer of 1912 for any news from Agent Hopkins, but it wasn't until 28 September that I began receiving a string of cables that documented on-going events. The first read: "Threats to Roosevelt's life in Los Angeles last week. Attributed by police to labor unions." The second arrived the next day: "In Atlanta, a Roosevelt supporter punched an agitated man bent on mounting the platform where TR stood." A week later, Hopkins wrote of a stenographer working for Roosevelt in Saginaw, Michigan, who threw a man into the street for rushing up to the Colonel. It was feared the stranger meant to do harm, though he claimed only to be seeking a handshake. Surely, I thought, with so many disruptions, there was just cause for the people protecting Roosevelt to anticipate additional assaults.

And in fact, the Colonel's people took precautions that appeared to go beyond the normal. In Chattanooga, Tennessee, for instance, thirty policemen were positioned at the auditorium where Roosevelt was speaking. In Chicago, Illinois, a troop of mounted police escorted the Colonel on his travels. In Racine, Wisconsin, a former soldier and bodyguard, promising to protect the former President, joined Roosevelt's entourage. For that matter, Roosevelt himself often carried a loaded revolver.

None of this, of course, revealed any proof that additional attacks had been thwarted or that any of these events were in some way tied to one another. As far as I could tell from Hopkins' reports, there appeared to be no specific evidence of some sinister organisation intent on assassinating a former President of the United States. In short, Theodore Roosevelt seemed as safe as any other politician presenting himself to the public.

Chapter Six

Once an order goes forth it can never be recalled.
That is one of the most necessary of our rules.
--Jack London
The Assassination Bureau, Ltd.

Upon Tuesday, 15 October 1912, the *New York Times* trumpeted the previous day's horror: "Maniac in Milwaukee Shoots Col. Roosevelt!" Here is a compilation of some other newspaper headings from across the United States: "Roosevelt Shot by Political Crank." "Col. Roosevelt Shot by Assassin." "Would-Be Assassin Shoots Col. Roosevelt." "Socialist in Milwaukee Shoots Roosevelt." "Roosevelt Shot."

On the surface, the unsuccessful assassin, described as a moon-faced German immigrant called John Schrank, appeared to be yet another lunatic acting on his own. As reported, his motives certainly sounded insane. Roosevelt must die, he had said, because by seeking a third Presidential term, the former President had broken a long-held tradition established by George Washington.

Even more disturbing was Schrank's hallucinatory tale of being paid a visit by the ghost of the assassinated President

William McKinley. McKinley's murder in 1900 had elevated Vice-President Roosevelt to the Presidency; and according to Schrank, the apparition—not unlike the ghost of Hamlet's father—had come to Schrank in the middle of the night many years before demanding vengeance. It was Roosevelt, the spectre said, not Czolgosz, who had assassinated McKinley; and for the past eleven years Schrank had been feeding on the spirit's desire for revenge.

The madman had dogged Roosevelt through much of the country and finally caught up to him in Milwaukee, Wisconsin. During the evening of 14 October, Roosevelt had dined at the Hotel Gilpatrick. Prior to the short drive to the Milwaukee Auditorium where he was to deliver a campaign speech, Roosevelt had stood up in the back of his open car to wave at a crowd of supporters. Having stationed himself some twelve feet from the machine, Schrank raised a .38 Colt revolver and fired once at the Colonel's chest. Immediately—before the would-be assassin could pull the trigger again—a man in Roosevelt's entourage leapt at the shooter and wrestled him to the ground.

As it turned out, the single bullet had indeed struck the former President, but the missile had first passed through the folded sheets of the Colonel's fifty-page speech, which had been wrapped round the former-President's glasses-case, all of which had been nesting in a breast pocket of his coat. By deflecting the bullet, the impediments saved Theodore Roosevelt's life.

Weakened and bloodied by the assault, he none the less went on to speak for eighty-minutes to a spellbound audience of ten thousand.

I read the newspapers closely. Of particular interest to me was the initial reaction of alienists to the shooter. It took little time to establish that Schrank was someone who kept very much to himself. Apparently, he used to drink beer alone in the back-room bar of his New York hotel (ironically called "The White House"). I could well imagine him sitting by himself in an out-of-the-way corner and, spurred on by his faith in ghosts, muttering threats against the former President. Perhaps someone had overheard his ravings. Perhaps some interested party had recognised in Schrank a malleable personality, a tractable sort who, without too much persuading, might be transformed into yet another "lone" gunman.

A few alienists, those obviously undaunted by raising questions of conspiracy, had gone so far as to posit some kind of subliminal hypnosis. In a susceptible state-of-mind, they asked, could not John Schrank have been beguiled into performing his dastardly act by a villain appearing to him in the guise of the murdered McKinley?

Such a line of questioning might yield precious results with a suspect able to identify his mesmeriser. But as long as Schrank knew nothing about the Assassination Bureau, he—like

Czolgosz, who had shot McKinley; Guiteau, who had shot Garfield; and Goldsborough, who had shot Phillips—could not direct the attention of the authorities back to the organisation.

Roosevelt himself may have detected the makings of a clandestine plot. Originally, the former President had planned to avoid the Gilpatrick by eating dinner in the *Mayflower*, his private railway car; but someone had decided that the hotel, where Schrank had just happened to position himself, offered a more welcoming venue. To his great misfortune, Roosevelt ultimately agreed to the change in plans, but not before questioning the decision.

It is also possible that Roosevelt saw in Schrank a puppet whose strings were controlled by unseen hands. Such a suspicion would explain the Colonel's extraordinary concern for the man who had just shot him. With angry citizens shouting death threats at the would-be assassin, Roosevelt was reported to have said to the police, "Don't hurt him . . . . See that no harm is done to him."

Certainly, Theodore Roosevelt, himself a former police commissioner of New York City, would understand that the death of the shooter while in custody would raise all sorts of suspicious questions about secret plots. That Schrank was not actually killed, however, did nothing in my mind to stifle the question of conspiracy. I am pleased to report that it also did not stifle the question in the mind of Sherlock Holmes.

The day after the attempt on Roosevelt's life, I received a wire from Holmes in Sussex. I confess to opening the yellow envelope with great anticipation. I was not disappointed.

"Convinced by shooting in Milwaukee," the telegram read. "Hope you have room for me. Arrive tomorrow."

*****

Not long after tea the next day, I discovered my wife with knit brows standing at the window of our sitting room. She had pulled the diaphanous curtain to the side and was peering through the glass into the gloom. I came up behind her to have a look and immediately understood her concern. A dismal portrait presented itself.

Beneath a darkened sky, a scruffy dustman was shuffling up the flags to our front door. His shaggy brown hair drooped from beneath a large dark hat, its brim covering most of his face. A long, brindled beard extended halfway down his soiled, baggy shirt; and his roomy, brown corduroy trousers, which were tied off at the knee, exposed a pair of well-worn boots.

Mrs Watson was duly put off. "John," said she in no uncertain terms, "tell that man to go round back where the dustbins are."

"Surely, Mrs Meeks should—"

"He'll be more inclined to remember such instructions if he hears them from the master of the house rather than from the housekeeper."

Dutifully, I opened the front door and pointed to the path leading behind the house.

"You there!" I called out. "The dustbins are at the back. Go round the side." And I pointed to the walkway leading to the rear of our residence.

The dustman stopped in his tracks, and it was only then that I noted the burgundy-coloured Gladstone he was carrying. He had placed it under his arm rather than holding it by the handles.

Slowly looking up at me, he pulled a saddened face. "Has it come to this, old fellow?" said a familiar voice. "Am I no longer welcome at your door?"

Surely, I can be forgiven. With little sun, the lighting was poor. Besides, what homeowner takes the time to scrutinise his workers' facial features? But, of course, once the presumed dustman removed his large hat and I could more carefully examine the face beneath the brown locks, I discerned what looked very much to me like the piercing grey eyes of Sherlock Holmes.

"Holmes," I queried, "is that you?"

"Ever the detective, Watson. I couldn't resist the urge to confront you in my work clothes."

"It was Mrs Watson you fooled," said I, attempting to cover my obtuseness. "It was she who issued the order to turn you away."

Holmes offered a brief chuckle, and I waved him in. As he passed me by and I wondered what had prompted such a deception, I could not help noticing the malodourous authenticity of his disguise. In truth, the stench reminded me of my meeting with Jack London back in Baker Street.

Much to the relief of Mrs Watson and myself, Holmes retired immediately to the room and washbasin we had prepared for him. Within a quarter hour, he reappeared sans aroma, brown wig and false beard; and my wife and I were staring at the familiar hawk-like nose and strong square chin of my old friend. To be sure, his natural hair contained more grey than I remembered, but then he might be thinking the same of mine.

"Gentlemen," said Mrs Watson placing two empty glasses before us, "I leave you to your pursuits."

I reached for the brandy decanter in the tantalus on the sideboard and mixed drinks for us with the sparkling water from the gasogene.

Holmes eyed the tiny bubbles rising to the top of the pale-brown liquid. "To Shinwell Johnson," said he, lifting his glass.

The toast surprised me enough to turn my face red. I had never mentioned to Holmes that I had gone to interview Johnson myself after the Morton-Watt shooting. Still, I managed to join him in clinking glasses and sampling the spirits.

"Why do you mention Shinwell?" I asked after an embarrassing silence.

"Upon my way here," said he sipping more of the brandy, "I took the occasion to look in at the Northumberland Arms. I fancied I might find him in residence there as I hoped to ask him a few questions about the Morton-Watt affair."

At this explanation my face flushed up a second time.

"And what do you know, Watson?" said Holmes with a dry chortle. "He told me he had had a meeting with *you* on the very subject not so long ago."

"Let me explain, Holmes. You see—"

"No explanation necessary, old fellow. You were correct on this matter; I was not. In fact, thanks to you, Johnson enabled me to discover a most intriguing piece of information."

"Thanks to *me*?"

"Quite so. Apparently, your questions prompted him to keep a keener ear to the ground. He correctly surmised that, whilst Wainwright had confessed to shooting Morton-Watt, there was more that needed to be examined. As a result, Johnson had his confederates keep their ears open for additional news.

Apparently, it didn't take long for them to confirm to Johnson that there had, in fact, been a woman who'd fired the additional round into Morton-Watt. What's more, they located her whereabouts."

Though this was very good news indeed, I none the less felt miffed. Such information should have been directed to *me*. After all, had I not been the first to speak to Johnson on this matter?

"Look here, Holmes. I gave the man my card. He was supposed to inform *me* if he learned anything new regarding the crime."

Holmes showed his teeth in a broad smile. "Ah, yes. It's funny what a bit of money can extract. As it turned out, it was a costly piece of information."

The thought of paying Shinwell Johnson had never crossed my mind. Justice alone should have been his reward. Hoping to conceal my latest round of *naiveté*, I returned to the main topic. "Where's the woman staying?"

"Oh, didn't I say? In a women's boarding house near Westminster Bridge on the other side of the river—much nicer accommodations, I might add, than a barmaid can afford."

"And let me guess. You somehow acquired the dustman's disguise—"

"Johnson had it among his costumes."

"And you rummaged in the dustbins of the establishment."

"Exactly! And after much laborious—and, I might add, distasteful—digging, I discovered *this*."

He passed me a slip of soiled white paper. It was folded neatly now, but bore the crimps and crinkles that clearly indicated its prior status as trash.

I eagerly opened it and observed the following brief text written in dark pencil: *MH, Friday.* The cryptic note could have meant anything, but given the sinister information passed along to us by Jack London—that Mycroft Holmes was to be a target of the Assassination Bureau and that the presumed assassin was currently abiding in London—we chose to err on the side of caution. As a result, one didn't have to be the world's first consulting detective to conclude that "MH" referred to Mycroft Holmes and that the action about to be undertaken—no less than an attempt on his life—was set to occur on Friday.

"Holmes!" I cried, waving the paper before him. "Friday's the day after tomorrow! But what time? Where? How?"

"Ah, Watson, you know how to ask the proper questions. Unfortunately, you sometimes also provide the answers. Thanks to those revelations in your report of the stolen submarine plans, most all the world knows *where* to find my brother."

Once again, my face had cause to turn red. In "The Bruce-Partington Plans," the sketch to which Holmes alluded and that I mentioned at the start of this narrative, I had reported the trinity of Mycroft's destinations—his lodgings in Pall Mall; his club, the Diogenes, across the road; and his office in Whitehall round the corner.

"What's more," Holmes added, "they also know *when* they can find him."

Holmes was right again. In my account describing the Greek interpreter to which I also referred at the start, I had recorded the precise time of Mycroft's stay at the Diogenes: from exactly 4.45 until exactly 7.40 every evening. So punctual was Mycroft that he had always put me in mind of the German philosopher Immanuel Kant, whose timing was said to be predictable enough for his neighbours to set their watches by the regularity of his daily walks through the streets of Königsberg. Holmes himself was fond of saying, "Not only does Mycroft follow his own rails, but he also maintains a timetable as reliable as Bradshaw's."

"I had no intention of placing your brother in any sort of peril," said I weakly.

Holmes waved away my guilt. "One cannot live in fear that one's every utterance will be appropriated by villains. We must focus on the present, old fellow. Mycroft's schedule may be known, but the specifics of where and how he might be assaulted while pursuing it requires further investigation."

"We don't have much time if an attack is scheduled for this Friday."

"Quite so, Watson."

"Might I suggest we begin by warning your brother of the danger he's in?"

"Much good it will do," Holmes snorted. "But I certainly agree that we must try. From now on, let the weight of the matter rest upon me."

*****

A taxi motored us to the Diogenes Club late Wednesday afternoon. As we exited the cab in the west end of Pall Mall, we were close enough to the clock tower at Westminster to hear the six o'clock chimes of Big Ben commence their toll.

"The exact time occurs with the first strike," Holmes pointed out as we approached the entrance. "When the city is quiet, the bells can be heard nine miles away."

Whilst I stood marvelling at Holmes' arcane knowledge, my friend submitted his card for Mycroft to Maypoole, the elderly doorman. The poor creature had to hold it close to his eyes to read the names.

We had been at the Diogenes before on not a few occasions, and yet the old man still said to my friend as if for verification: "You are the younger brother." Only after receiving a nod, did he allow us to tiptoe our way across the black-and-white chequerboard-tiled floor and up the stairs to the chamber called the Stranger's Room, the single location in the club where talking was permitted. Its being between 4.45 and 7.40, there was no doubt that Mycroft would be in attendance. In fact, there was no other establishment so appealing to him.

As most of my readers will recall, the Diogenes Club was founded by a number of gentlemen—Mycroft included—who sought a gathering place in which to exhibit asocial behaviour, foremost of which was silence. No talking was allowed virtually anywhere on the premises, a proposition that greatly appealed to the older brother of Sherlock Holmes.

After a number of quiet minutes, the man himself appeared. I hadn't seen Mycroft Holmes in years. Though like his younger brother's, Mycroft's hair had turned a great deal more grey, his movements looked as ponderous and unhurried as they had years before. Thanks to his ample figure, he still moved at the same slow pace.

Following a formal exchange of greetings, Mycroft allowed himself to sink into a soft brown-leather chair by the bow window that overlooked the sidewalks of Pall Mall. Night was beginning to cloak the city; and from his stationary vantage, Mycroft could observe the frantic Londoners scurrying home to their dinners or other points of *rendezvous*.

The older brother, of course, was much more than mere observer. Sherlock Holmes had always maintained that Mycroft's mind was every bit as sharp as his own. If pressed, he might have admitted, "Even sharper." Thus, Holmes had no need for small talk prior to laying out to his brother the case for conspiracy.

My friend began by explaining how we had originally learned of and immediately discounted Jack London's account of the Assassination Bureau; how, despite an ever-growing list of victims like David Graham Phillips and King Edward himself, not even the subsequent murder of Charles Morton-Watt could convince Sherlock Holmes of the Bureau's malicious existence; how it was not until the attempted assassination of Theodore Roosevelt a few days earlier that Holmes had admitted he had finally come to accept the horrifying truth.

"For years, Mycroft," said he, "for decades, in fact, a malignant organisation has perfunctorily been carrying out the assassinations of influential figures that it deems antagonistic to the common good. Worse, for whatever the reason, they now have *you* in their crosshairs."

Mycroft exploded with a burst of laughter. "*Et tu, frater?*" said he, slowly shaking his head. "Do you really think we haven't fully investigated the death of the King, Sherlock? Not to mention the Roosevelt shooting in Milwaukee. The man Schrank was a complete nutter. For God's sake, gentlemen, he claimed the ghost of William McKinley had implored him to shoot the chap! We've had the testimony cabled to us. The man actually stated that McKinley's ghost had pointed an accusatory finger at a phantom Roosevelt! This Schrank went about stalking his target across the American landscape, and he fired a bullet at Roosevelt when he finally had him in his sights—all because of spirits and ghosts. *Fairy tales,* Sherlock."

My friend emitted an exasperated sigh.

"Oh," continued Mycroft, "I've seen the Coroner's report about a second shooter in the Morton-Watt affair. But in Schrank's case, there's no one to pick up the slack. The American authorities discovered no connections to any outside groups and are quite convinced that the man acted on his own. From what Whitehall have learned, there's no reason to doubt that interpretation. Yet now I find my own *brother* swallowing the fantasy of some *über*-organisation that seems bent on eliminating public figures willy-nilly. My word, Sherlock; I expected more from you."

I had never heard Holmes dressed down so. Fortunately, however, his brother's harsh words could not side-track my friend.

"Whatever you may think of my reasoning," said Holmes, "promise me that through Friday at the very least you will vary your ever-so-predictable routine. Take new rooms for a short time. Avoid your club. Change your work hours. I know that you're a creature of habit, brother-mine, but such variations in your daily programme might just save your life."

"Absolutely *not*, Sherlock!" countered Mycroft, shaking his head in dismay. "If I am, as you say, 'a creature of habit', it is because *not* having to think about the trivial—my travels, my schedule, my rooms—allows me to concentrate my full faculties on matters of primary importance to the state. I refuse to jeopardise the welfare of the nation by diluting my intellectual capacity. Furthermore, my decision is final!" With a quick nod of his head, he added, "Good day, gentlemen"; and after rising with some difficulty, he proceeded to march out of the room, his chin held high in defiance.

"I suppose, Watson," said Holmes, "that we shall have to save his life in spite of his obstinacy."

Sherlock Holmes also rose, and I followed him down the stairs and back across the chequerboard to the exit of the Diogenes Club. Stepping out of the silence and into the hubbub of London traffic, we re-entered the world of reality.

*****

To his credit, Mycroft finally did capitulate to a pair of his brother's requests: he agreed to our searching his rooms and club for explosives, and he agreed to let a rotating series of constables shadow him. With the aide of Inspector MacKinnon, Holmes would be allowed to place a policeman at a respectful distance from the doors of Mycroft's rooms throughout the night and have the constable accompany Mycroft at an equally respectful distance for his morning walk to Whitehall. Another constable would assume the role during Mycroft's afternoon return and his subsequent journey across the road to his club.

As long as Mycroft's schedule went undisturbed, he agreed not to complain. Oh, he grumbled at first about the foolish waste of police resources; but concluding that it would be easier to accept the policeman than to continue arguing with his brother, he acquiesced. Perhaps, he might even have taken some comfort in the belief that, if rumours about the Assassination Bureau turned out to be true, a uniformed constable might be just the thing to frighten off any would-be assassins.

*****

The clock was ticking, as it were; and the next day we journeyed back to Northumberland Street to revisit Shinwell Johnson. We had purposely waited for lunchtime in order to find the man at his favourite table in the Northumberland Arms. At the rear of the establishment, we espied him easily enough; and with a wave of his half-eaten ham sandwich, he motioned us to join him. We all shook hands like old friends, and Holmes and I sat down at his table. Our banter carried on for a few minutes, and I began to wonder if Shinwell had forgot his concerns about being observed socializing with defenders of the law.

"You're not worried," I asked him, "that someone might see you mixing with the likes of us?"

Johnson hoisted his tankard of Guinness. "It's just gone noon," said he, taking a long pull. "Not so suspicious a crowd."

Even so, it was obvious how, informant that he was, he still feared being overheard. He pushed the tankard aside as he leaned forward and spoke to Holmes in a near whisper.

"She calls herself Maisie Trilling though she's Russian by birth and linked to Socialists and anarchists. Her Russian name's Grunya—so they say—and she's young, probably in her early twenties. One of m' mates saw her serving beer at the Northumberland and recognised her from a previous job."

"The Modern Woman," I mumbled scornfully.

"Right about that, Doctor," said Johnson, failing once more to appreciate the sweet contrast.

"How's she going to do it?" Holmes asked. "Gun or bomb?"

"Don't know for certain, Mr Holmes, but Mercer saw her enter the bicycle shop."

"'Mercer', you say?" repeated my friend, nodding slowly. "That's good."

Since the turn of the century, Mercer, like Johnson, had served as a member of Holmes' so-called agency. I did not know the man since he had been hired since my departure from Baker Street. But he had provided Holmes with many a sound lead like his description of Dorak in the Commercial Road, which helped Holmes solve the singular mystery of the so-called "creeping man".

"Nothing else to report, gentlemen," said Johnson softly. He took a quick bite of what was left of his sandwich before adding in the same quiet voice, "Hope I've been of some help to you."

Holmes passed the informant a coin that flashed golden as it caught the light. "That should also cover the cost of the dustman's clothes," Holmes added, "which I took the liberty to burn."

Then Holmes and I both pushed our chairs back and rose to leave.

"Ta," said Shinwell Johnson. With a fraternal wink, he saluted my friend with his tankard.

"A bicycle shop?" I asked as soon as we were outside. "Any such shop in particular?"

"Come, I'll show you. It's not far, but in the interest of time, we'll hire a cab."

*****

Holmes hailed a taxi; and traveling north via Kingsway and Southampton Row, we turned left into Great Russell Street and found ourselves among the numerous other cabs on their approach to the British Museum.

Before we reached that grand edifice, however, Holmes shouted, "Here!" to our driver, and we stopped before reaching Montague Street. Only after Holmes paid the fare, and we exited the cab, did he point to a small establishment just beyond the turning. A sign with white lettering on black background read "Cooper Bros. Bicycles—Hospital and Sales—Ten Years at this Location."

I confess to being ignorant on the specifics of such transports, but I must say that so far as I could see the shop offered no great mystery. A few new cycles stood outside the building along with placards advertising various brands like B.S.A., Rudge-Whitworth, and Raleigh. Additional signs promoted various tricycles; Michelin, Dunlop and Palmer pneumatic tyres; and all manner of "expert repairs".

The interior looked normal as well. In addition to a few ancient penny-farthings, lots of shiny, new machines waiting to be sold stood next to one another like a line of dominoes—push one, and they all fall down. A number of unattached wheels and solitary frames hung from large metal hooks on the wall.

A salesman in a dark waistcoat and protruding white sleeves approached us. "May I interest you gentlemen in a new cycle?" he asked from behind an unctuous smile.

"Actually, we'd like to see Mr Malchikov," Holmes replied.

The man's smile faded. "Oh, is he working on a bicycle for you?"

"In a manner of speaking."

The salesman pointed in the direction of a door next to a stack of tyres. It bore a sign announcing "Official Repairs".

"Who is this Malchikov?" I asked Holmes once the salesman was out of earshot. "For that matter, what are we doing in a bicycle shop?"

"Sorry, Watson, didn't I say? Kazimir Malchikov is an anarchist bomb-maker."

A bomb-maker? I just had time to take in that bit of information before we entered the backroom, a workspace for bicycle repairs. Like the showroom we had exited, here too were bicycles, only far fewer in number and in various stages of disarray. Some lacked wheels, other saddles, and a few were turned upside down to allow easy access to their nether parts. These machines weren't as shiny as those for sale; and as one would expect, spots of black oil and grease covered the nearby workbenches and the assorted rags that were lying about. At least, there were no bombs on display!

For some reason, I had expected to encounter a grey-haired, veteran mechanic at work, but what I saw was a young man who could not have been much older than twenty. Holding an oilcan, he was stooped over an inverted bicycle and applying a black, viscous liquid to the pedals. He wore a stain-covered leather apron and a dark, corduroy flat-cap. Coils of greasy hair hung down to his shoulders, and he looked up at us with dark, penetrating eyes. He remained silent, however.

"Mr Malchikov," said Holmes at last.

"You come for bicycle?" asked the mechanic in Russian-accented English

"No, we've come to see you concerning your *other* occupation."

Malchikov put down the oilcan and continued to stare. A minatory atmosphere began to darken the workroom.

"I have no interest at present in reporting you to the police," said Holmes strategically. "They already know of your existence and are merely waiting to catch you in the act."

"Please, go," said Malchikov. "You are bad for work."

"Is that what you told Maisie Trilling when she came here to see you?"

Malchikov didn't answer immediately. Finally, he said, "I don't know what you mean."

"The Russian woman," said Holmes, "we know she was here. We know what she intends to do. We simply need your confirmation."

"I tell you nothing." He picked up a dirty towel and wiped his hands with it. One of his blackened fingers popped through a hole. "Now you go, or I call for help."

Holmes stared at the towel. I suspected he feared it concealed a spanner or screwdriver that Malchikov intended to throw at us.

"Good day then," said Holmes. "I thank you for your time. Actually, this visit has been most helpful indeed."

The Russian looked at my friend with knotted brow and quizzical eyes.

Offering a slight smile, Holmes turned and exited the workroom; I followed him all the way out of the shop.

"I thought you gave up rather quickly," said I when we had reached the pavement. "What did you mean when you said the man had been 'helpful'?"

"I found out what I needed to know, Watson. Did you not notice the rag?"

"The rag? Do you mean the filthy towel he was holding?"

"I grant you that the 'rag', as you called it, was spotted with oil stains; but amidst them all, one could discern a tiny, embroidered shield containing the red and yellow vertical bars of the Northumberland Arms. In its previous life, Watson, that 'rag' served as a towel where Maisie Trilling had worked—and if the aperture is any sort of witness, possibly the very towel in which she'd hidden the pistol and through which she'd fired the shot that struck Charles Morton-Watt in the back. I imagine she expected Malchikov to dispose of the thing. Instead, he casually put it to use in his repair shop."

"And still you believe she purchased a bomb from this bicycle mechanic?"

"I do indeed. It is as I expected. Malchikov's no maker of guns or a chemist who conjures poisons; and to the best of our knowledge, *she* is no cyclist. Why else bother to meet with a bomb-maker than to secure some sort of infernal device? There is no doubt that the Assassination Bureau has the financial means to meet his price. Besides, we don't have much time. It is the only— and, therefore, the best—theory we have to work with."

"Then should we not alert Scotland Yard to this fellow?"

"What I told Malchikov earlier is true. They know of his existence though they have yet to catch him in the act."

"But what about your brother? Doesn't this information confirm he's in imminent danger?"

"Mycroft has a guard. We know that the attack is supposed to occur tomorrow. Thanks to our visit to the bicycle shop, we can assume the type of weapon—a bomb. In point of fact, we can assume a *timed* device. One doesn't depend on a craftsman like Malchikov for a simple stick of dynamite."

"Then let us find Mycroft," said I, "and insist that he alter his daily schedule."

"Ah, Watson," said Sherlock Holmes shaking his head, "if only it were that simple."

Holmes stood in the background whilst I hailed a taxi, and the two of us began the drive back to my house in Queen Anne Street. Holmes sat with his long fingers steepled. It was a pose I associated with the focusing of his concentration.

Suddenly, he leaned forward, "A detour south!" he commanded the driver. "To the London Library in St. James's Square!"

Now I had no idea of the purpose for such a trip. The library in question, a book-lending institution for paying members, was a half-hour's walk from our old rooms; and Holmes and I would frequently amble down Bond Street to St. James's Square to take advantage of the library's various collections.

"I need to ask a favour of your old friend Lomax, the sub-librarian," said Holmes in response to my quizzical expression.

Over the years I had seen Lomax only occasionally. Our meetings increased in frequency, however, when some recent investigations involved a number of celebrated authors. I turned to Lomax when I sought the novels of writers like Mark Twain, Stephen Crane, and Joseph Conrad.

Attentive readers may also remember that it was Lomax who had offered help in the previously-noted case called "The "Illustrious Client". Lomax was the librarian who had furnished me the volume regarding Chinese pottery that I devoted hour after hour to reading. With Holmes' encouragement, I had foolishly believed that cramming up would allow me to dupe Baron Gruner, a *connoisseur* of such art. Today, however, I had no idea what my friend might be seeking from Lomax.

Holmes asked me to wait in the motor as we approached the grey stone library in St. James's Square. No sooner did we stop than he sprang to the pavement and rushed through the arched entrance. He must have easily located the aforementioned sub-librarian, for he returned to the taxi just a few minutes later. He was carrying a thick volume with burgundy-coloured covers; I immediately recognised it as a 1908 edition of *Chambers' English Dictionary*.

"You didn't need to stop here for a copy of *Chambers*," said I. "There's one on the desk in my study."

Sherlock Holmes responded with a smile. "I know," he replied cryptically.

We arrived at my house shortly thereafter.

Chapter Seven

A man with a club is a law-maker.
--Jack London
The Call of the Wild

Beneath a darkening sky, Sherlock Holmes set off on his own for Scotland Yard. He had matters to arrange with Mr MacKinnon, he said, and told me not to be alarmed if he returned very late that night—or not all.

Before leaving, he added, "If it's not too much of an imposition, old fellow, might we start with a *café noir* at four o'clock tomorrow morning?"

"Four o'clock?" I responded with surprise. Generally speaking, Holmes himself was a late riser. Not that I minded the occasional early wake-up when duty called. I clearly remembered being knocked up by Holmes early one morning in the investigation I titled "The Speckled Band", but that had been at a mere quarter-past-seven.

Holmes' stern look betokened disapproval of my reaction. "Tomorrow's *Friday*, Watson—the day of reckoning according to Maisie Trilling's scrap of paper. I intend to be at Mycroft's rooms at the break of dawn. We shall require the strong coffee for stimulation before entering the fray. Besides, tell me a better time to go seeking an assassin."

Needless to say, I wondered what type of last-minute arrangements regarding Mycroft's safety required all-night preparations. Whatever his intentions, I thought that waiting till the night before the deadline to make final a plan seemed very risky indeed. Still, it was about his own brother that Holmes was worrying, and I expected he would take every precaution at whatever o'clock was necessary.

Even then, however, I remembered with regret the early-morning starts to some of our investigations that had got Mrs Hudson out of bed. As a consequence, I had no intention of summoning Mrs Meeks at the ungodly hour that Holmes had requested. All I asked was for her to leave the coffee tin on the sideboard.

*****

Friday morning.

I have never been a sound sleeper; but with Mycroft's life at stake, I spent more of the night than usual marking the hours as they slowly crept past. *What is Holmes up to?* I wondered. *What does the coming day hold in store?*

I rose early enough to prepare the coffee—early enough to set bread, butter, and strawberry jam on the dining room table as well. Oh, I knew full well that Holmes was wont to skip his breakfast on days a case preoccupied him, but I needed to do something to engage my time whilst waiting for him.

Holmes had warned that he might not return during the night, and he was true to his word. It was a quarter to four that morning when I heard the key at the front-door-lock.

"Where have you been?" I asked when he entered the dining room. His face was flushed; his breathing was rapid; and in spite of the coolness of the weather, he was perspiring freely. I could but wonder what nocturnal activity had rendered him thus.

"In a moment," he greeted me. Then, without so much as removing his coat, he poured himself a cup of coffee.

"Are you all right?" I asked.

He slapped my question away with a wave of his hand.

"Do you want to sit?"

"No time," he answered, sampling the hot brew between quick breaths.

Following his example, I too remained standing and sipped my coffee.

Holmes savoured his drink for a moment, then moved towards the table and the bits of food I had laid out.

"There are aspects of Mycroft's behaviour," said he, lathering a slice of bread with jam, "of which I think you're not aware. And I'm trying to take them into consideration."

"For instance?"

"'For instance', his infamous punctuality. You've never indicated how he establishes the correct time."

"I suppose I've never thought about it."

"Quite so, Watson, but think of it you must when the man's life is in jeopardy. How do you imagine he sets his watch?"

I shrugged my shoulders.

"By the striking of Big Ben in the tower at Westminster," said he between bites. "It's most convenient since his limited peregrinations never take him beyond the sound of its chimes. The clock is said to be accurate within a single second of the official time recorded in Greenwich; and as a result, so is Mycroft. People have been known to set their watches by the preciseness of his schedule."

Kant and that clock tower in Königsberg again.

"Whenever he leaves his rooms in the morning, he does so on the quarter hour past seven, and he never fails to adjust his watch if it is only a minute different from the clock in the tower."

"But if Mycroft still insists on refusing to vary his schedule, how does whatever o'clock it is pertain to today's activities?"

"That, my friend, remains to be seen. Right now, in fact."

I'm sure I had no idea what he was talking about, but I followed his lead when he put down his cup and turned towards the door.

"I'll just be a moment," I said. "I need my coat."

"While you're at it," offered Holmes, "bring along your revolver. Who knows whom we might run into during today's adventure?"

I nodded and, retrieving my Webley No. 2 from the desk in my study, grabbed my heavy coat and joined Holmes outside. Early as it was that Friday morning, it was also dark and foggy; and cabs were scarce. With Holmes pacing nervously on the pavement, I suggested we walk the short distance to the Langham Hotel where taxis always seemed available. Within five minutes, we were seated in a cab at the head of the short queue in Portland Place.

"Pall Mall!" Holmes barked at the driver.

The motor's lights bounced off the thick fog as we drove through a shrouded London. So thick was the mist curling round the walls of Mycroft's lodgings that we found it difficult to discern the outer door. Indeed, after alighting from the cab, we could barely make out the constable who, like a ghost among the feathery tendrils, was trodding back and forth on the pavement before the entrance.

Holmes and I immediately crossed the road, hiding ourselves behind the corner of the Diogenes Club. It was a perfect vantage point for keeping our eyes on Mycroft's front door though not even the large building itself could protect us from the cold air. I took comfort in the warmth of my ulster, but I must concede that the pistol in my pocket made me feel more secure.

At first, we heard nothing beyond the constable's muffled footfalls. Within a few minutes, however, we also heard the tolling of the five o'clock hour from Big Ben and the additional rings from the lesser bells at each quarter hour. The 5.45 chimes were accompanied by the rise of a hazy sun, for the overcast that had characterised most of the early fall that year seemed intent on blanketing this October day as well.

Not that there was much to see when the light finally did arrive and the fog began to dissipate. With the constable still on his march, it seemed reasonable to assume that no one had penetrated Mycroft's rooms during the night. In fact, it seemed safe to conclude that not until Mycroft began the trek to his office would he appear a target for any covert evil-doer.

At last, minutes after the chimes from Westminster marked 7.15, the man himself emerged on the street. By then, most of the fog had disappeared, and we could easily discern his imposing figure. His heavy black coat with its astrakhan collar and cuffs made him loom even larger than usual, and under his arm nestled a battered leather briefcase. He took a step or two forward and then—just as Holmes had reported—he paused to check his ever-accurate pocket watch.

On this occasion, however, Mycroft frowned and, after leaning the briefcase against his leg, employed both hands to regulate the silver timepiece—holding it in one, setting it with the other. Task completed, he picked up the briefcase, looked up and down the street, and plodded off towards Whitehall. The constable, who had halted his pacing when Mycroft first stopped, issued an informal salute as Mycroft passed him and fell in a few steps behind.

Mycroft acted as if he was late, employing a gait that seemed positively rapid by his usual standards. Still, he moved slowly—slowly enough to allow us to follow him with ease on the opposite side of the street, slowly enough to render himself an easy mark to anyone perched nearby. Indeed, however much we might have expected to encounter an explosive device, our eyes scoured the surrounding windows in search of an isolated rifle barrel as well. At the same time, we had to study the people walking towards him. Nor could we discount the passing motor-cars or carriages from which a bomb might be tossed.

Only when Mycroft finally entered the white-stone government building that housed his office did Holmes and I breathe more easily. It defied belief, we agreed, that an organisation—even one as practised in the black arts as the Assassination Bureau was reputed to be—would risk penetrating heavily-guarded government grounds when more benign locations were so readily available.

Once Mycroft was safely ensconced inside, Holmes and I retraced our steps back to his rooms and searched the premises for any lethal devices. Only after we assured ourselves that there were none, did we perform the same service across the road in the Diogenes, learning from a porter who spoke with us in the Strangers' Room, which chair was Mycroft's favourite and where he liked to dine. As methodical as Holmes was in his scrutiny, however, we were as unsuccessful in the club as we had been in Mycroft's rooms and returned to Whitehall empty-handed.

The clock had already struck 4.00, and the sky was still light when Mycroft Holmes, wrapped in his great coat once more and carrying his briefcase, exited the government building. During his return to Pall Mall, the same protective measures performed that morning began again. A new constable immediately accompanied Mycroft as he moved along Whitehall, and we repeated our surreptitious surveillance of the street around him.

At this time of day, however, a major difference presented itself. In the afternoon there were far more individuals of whom to be wary. What's more, on so chilly a day, the many pedestrians scuttling about in their heavy coats and protective scarves and hats provided an endless array of suspects who might be concealing a weapon. Even so, I mused, it was not as cold as winter, and the precautions of the young blonde woman coming into view whose hands resided within a dark fur muff seemed excessive.

The half-hour struck a few minutes before Mycroft reached his rooms; and looking at his watch again, he frowned once more and paused to reset the timepiece a second time that day. He remained inside just long enough to discard his briefcase and then, still in his great coat, re-emerged and, obviously late, crossed the road for the Diogenes at as quick a pace as he could muster.

Leaving his police shadow behind, Mycroft nodded at Maypoole, the ageing doorman, and—much to our relief—safely entered the club. After all, we had checked the premises earlier; certainly, he would be safe during his stay within. For close to three restless hours, Holmes and I, our eyes fixed on the great oak door at the entrance, stood waiting in the shadows for Mycroft to re-appear. If Nemesis was destined to strike that day, Nemesis was running out of time.

At last, the chimes struck 7.30, and I glanced at my watch to verify the time. Strangely, it seemed to be running slow, and I readjusted it. As expected, at exactly 7.40 Mycroft, wrapped in his great coat, appeared. Carrying a folded newspaper under his arm, he stopped at a nearby tobacconist's kiosk and purchased a cigar, which he proceeded to light. Pausing for a moment to exhale the smoke, he stood observing the tiny cloud dissipate round him.

"Come on, come on," Sherlock Holmes muttered, and I thought he was talking to his brother.

Suddenly, a tremendous roar erupted, and the ground beneath us shook.

A huge explosion tore through the Diogenes Club, causing its very walls to shudder. A window to the right of the outer door blew out, and a long tongue of flame leapt up through the gaping hole.

His cigar gone flying, Mycroft was blown backward onto the pavement, cushioned perhaps by the folds of his coat. Within seconds a handful of his fellow-club members staggered out through the front door. Instinctively, I had reached for my pistol—but to no avail. Whatever damage there was had already occurred.

I stood transfixed. Holmes, however, sprang into action, dashing across the road—not to his stricken brother, as one might expect, or even to the door of the club—but towards the blonde woman with the muff, who had strangely just reappeared and now stood not ten paces from where Mycroft had fallen. Her right hand was still encased in the fur; but Holmes grabbed her wrist and, twisting, forced her to drop the revolver I could now see she was trying to extract.

In an image of viciousness that I shall not soon forget, she drew back her red lips in a snarl of animal ferocity, exposed her sharp, dagger-like teeth, and attempted to bite Holmes' hand. By now, however, the constable had reached the pair and aided Holmes in subduing the vixen. I joined them seconds later, and Inspector MacKinnon arrived immediately thereafter. Within moments, the woman was braceleted and taken to Scotland Yard.

Chapter Eight

Law is one thing and right is another thing.
Ask any lawyer.
--Jack London
The Iron Heel

In an uncharacteristic but heart-warming display of emotion, Sherlock Holmes draped his arm round the shoulder of his obviously rattled brother and gently guided him to Mycroft's bachelor's quarters across the road.

I followed the two brothers into the same sitting room we had searched the previous day. As yesterday, it appeared an unassuming chamber full of the weighty books, wrinkled newspapers, and crumpled stationery one would associate with the tireless government worker Mycroft was known to be.

Through the front window we could see the fire brigade dousing the few remaining flames and hear shouts from the police ordering people about. Fascinating as the scene was, we managed to usher the ashen-faced Mycroft away from the glass, and soon the three of us were drinking whisky and water in hopes of soothing our rattled nerves.

For more than an hour, we sat with our drinks in hushed contemplation before a knock on the door commanded our attention. It was Inspector MacKinnon.

"I trust you're all right, sir," said he to Mycroft upon entering. "With your permission, I've come to offer my report— such as it is."

Mycroft gestured at an empty chair.

At the arrival of the policeman, Holmes had lit a cigarette, but my friend was anything but calm. "What of the woman with the gun?" he asked before MacKinnon could say another word. The vehemence with which Holmes exhaled a cloud of smoke signified his impatience.

"'The woman with the gun'?" repeated the Inspector slowly as he sat down. "Ah, yes, the woman with the gun." He produced a small notebook, which he consulted from time to time as he described the lady in question.

"Her name is Maisie Trilling. Russian by birth. About twenty-five years old."

Holmes and I exchanged glances. The description of the woman in custody matched what we had already heard from Shinwell Johnson.

"She grew up here in England," MacKinnon continued, "and has no accent. She claims to be employed by her father, but she refused to name any sort of business he's connected with. She gets offered various jobs and is paid when the jobs are done—no questions asked. She declined to tell us what kind of jobs; and besides her small role in it, she said she knows nothing about the organisation her father runs. Envelopes containing her instructions and payments are sent through the post. She was quite cooperative, really—without telling us a bloody thing."

Sherlock Holmes stared at the Inspector.

"I need not add, Mr Holmes, that she expressed no understanding of why she was accosted by you in the street. Or, for that matter, arrested by me."

"Of course not," murmured Holmes.

MacKinnon took a deep breath and patted his moustache. He seemed to be stalling for time. "Unfortunately," he announced at last, "we were forced to release her."

Holmes, his brother and I all gasped at the same time.

"You see, gentlemen, whatever the crimes of which she might be suspected, she lives under the shield of British law. Without any connections convincingly made between her and either the Morton-Watt shooting at the Old Bell Tavern or the outrage across the road, we had to let her go."

"But the *gun*!" I protested. "Surely—"

"At the very least, Doctor, we were hoping to charge her with illegal possession of a firearm, but let us not forget that she never actually shot at anyone. What's more, not only did she produce a gun licence, which she had recently purchased from a post office; but she also presented a statement signed by a Justice of the Peace that she was planning to be out of the country for at least six months—she's bound for Serbia, I believe. Such travel plans—as you may know—also allow her to possess such a weapon. I'm afraid that with no link to the bombing, we had no grounds for detaining her."

Holmes leaned forward, prepared to probe more deeply; but Mycroft interrupted, offering MacKinnon a whisky, which the Inspector declined. Instead he sat turning his bowler round and round in his hands. He began to speak again only after Mycroft addressed him directly.

"What have you learned of the bombing itself?" Mycroft asked.

In response, the policeman waved his hat at the window through which we had been staring at the flame-streaked Diogenes Club. "As you can see, gentlemen," said he, "the bomb exploded in the foyer of the building. It had a timing device; and as best we could surmise from the remains of the mechanism, it exploded at precisely 7.35."

"Impossible," observed Mycroft. "At 7.35 I was examining the newspapers on my way to the front door for my 7.40 exit. 7.35 is when I always peruse the daily papers I haven't read in the club so I can transport the interesting ones back here." He indicated a brown-leather ottoman near his desk that was stacked high with old newspapers. "I often spend some four or five minutes at the rack scanning the papers for engaging stories to savour later. Someone obviously knew that I always stand there for a few minutes prior to leaving in order to decide which papers to bring home. Had the bomb exploded five minutes earlier, I would have been a dead man."

"Fortunately," said I, "the timing must have been off."

"Equally fortunate," added Mycroft, "no one else was nearby when the bloody thing exploded."

"Right you are, sir," replied MacKinnon. "The old doorman was posted outside. No one was hurt. We may thank God for that."

"Though indeed," said Mycroft, "the bomb made a mighty sound."

"Such a narrow escape," I observed. "It is truly something to contemplate—a life saved by blind luck."

Holmes placed his cigarette in a nearby glass ashtray and offered a brief smile. "Not quite blind luck, I'm afraid," said he. "And certainly *not* God's work."

I had no clue to his meaning, but the pleasure he displayed in rubbing his hands together suggested that in some singular manner he himself must have been responsible for safeguarding his brother.

"What are you saying, Holmes?" I asked.

"Do you recall, Watson, that I informed you of how Mycroft sets his watch according to the clock in the Westminster tower?"

"As I *do*," Mycroft confirmed whilst I nodded in agreement.

"As well one should," said Holmes, "for its mechanism is unusually precise. The attendants in the clock room receive hourly telegraphic signals from the observatory in Greenwich and are thus continually able to monitor the clock's accuracy."

"I had no idea," said I.

"Oh, yes," my friend replied, picking up his cigarette again. "We Holmeses are a punctual lot—obstinate, perhaps, but punctual."

"Obvious on both counts," I observed. "So what did you do?"

Holmes inhaled the cigarette smoke, and whilst holding his breath, still was able to offer, "It is as the Turks say." Exhaling, he pronounced, "*'Dağ sana gelmezse, sen dağa gideceksin'.*"

I looked puzzled.

"'If the mountain won't come to you', Watson, 'then you must go to the mountain.' I couldn't get Mycroft to change his punctual ways, so I decided instead to interfere with the clock. I sped it up."

"Ah," MacKinnon sighed. "Now I understand."

I'm afraid that I didn't. In fact, all I could do for the moment was simply to stare at Holmes in amazement.

"You—you—" I finally managed to sputter, *"—you sped up the clock?"* A fantastic image came to mind of Holmes dangling from one of the bronze hands in the giant clock's face some one-hundred-eighty feet in the air as he tried to pull it faster. *"How? How on earth could you accomplish such a feat?"*

"I actually got the idea from a century-old rumour. You know how productive I consider the knowledge of antecedent crimes, Watson. No doubt, you've heard of the *Zytglogge,* the clock tower in Bern."

I shook my head in ignorance.

"Sorry," said he. "I should have used the standard German *Zeitglocke* instead of the Bernese. Still no recollection?"

Again I shook my head.

"Well, though Swiss authorities have never confirmed the story, a murder was said to have been committed in 1814 in Bern's *Stadtplatz.* According to legend, the target, a government official, was separated from his guards because the villains were able to speed up the clock mechanism in the tower. No less an authority than Hans Dichter refers to the case in his *Annals of Continental Crime.*"

"I—I never heard of such a thing," said I.

"Oh, it's all there in my commonplace book, Watson, under the letter "B".

I could well imagine that Holmes had collected such information about a clock tower in Bern, but that he could recall so much of it when needed was an inestimable skill.

"Do you remember when I was out all night?"

Still stupefied, I could barely bring myself to nod.

"After I left you, I stopped in at Scotland Yard to see Mr MacKinnon."

The policeman now picked up the story. "You see, gentlemen, Mr Holmes asked me to contact the Home Office. In the name of protecting Mr Mycroft Holmes, he wanted them to approve the silencing of those hourly Greenwich telegraphic signals. For the life of me, I couldn't see the connection at the time."

"With Mycroft's life at stake," explained Holmes, "I assumed the government would honour the Inspector's request. I didn't ask for more assistance because I didn't have the time for them to stage a debate. Besides, I wasn't certain they'd actually approve the rest of my plan."

"Quite right," agreed MacKinnon. "Silencing the signals is one thing; allowing someone to monkey with the clock itself is quite another."

"From the Yard," Holmes continued, "I dashed along Whitehall to the clock tower and reached the entrance in less than ten minutes. The tower was closed, of course, but it wasn't difficult to crack the lock. It's not as if they're expecting anyone to break in, after all. Once inside, it was child's play to find the closet containing uniforms of the workmen who attend the clock itself."

"All highly irregular," frowned MacKinnon, pulling at his moustache again. "I hadn't any idea of exactly what you were up to. It's small wonder you private detectives gain credit for uncovering clues the police can't get at."

Throughout this banter, I was still struggling to come to terms with the enormity of Holmes' plan. *"You sped up the clock?"* I repeated in disbelief.

Holmes smiled. "I spent most all of the night in the tower. After I had put on a uniform, I proceeded to climb the spiral stairway—a very *steep* spiral stairway, I should add."

"Surely, not to the *top*, Holmes! Good heavens! It's little wonder you looked winded when you returned this morning."

My friend allowed himself a brief chuckle. "It's three-hundred-thirty-four stone steps to the belfry, Watson, but fortunately I didn't have to climb quite that high. I was merely aiming for the top of the pendulum in the central shaft."

"My word," I gasped.

Holmes beamed proudly.

"The ascent is truly exhilarating. I began my climb near the sandbags at the bottom. They're in place so the clock-weights will hit something soft if they fall. When I had got about a third of the way up—at least, I had counted more than a hundred steps—I discovered the decorated prison suites they reserve for unruly MP's. After another hundred or so—what I reckoned was more than halfway—I paused for a few moments. I must confess that I was feeling a bit light-headed—probably from hauling the extra weight."

"Extra weight?" MacKinnon asked.

"But I knew I had to carry on," said Holmes, ignoring the query, "and once I passed the clock weights, I knew I could make the distance to the top of the pendulum."

"What extra weight were you carrying?" MacKinnon persisted.

Holding up his forefinger for additional time, Holmes proceeded with his explanation in the most didactic fashion. "A small doughnut-shaped tray caps the pendulum, and in reality coins are occasionally placed upon it to regulate the accuracy of the clock. You see, placing a penny, which weighs a bit more that one-tenth of an ounce, atop the thing raises the pendulum's centre of gravity. The result is to increase the speed of the pendulum's arc four-tenths of a second in twenty-four hours. According to my figures, ten pennies would speed it up four seconds—one-hundred-fifty pennies, sixty seconds. Seven-hundred-fifty pennies would speed it up five minutes.

"In plain English, gentlemen, I reckoned it would require a little less than six pounds of weight to increase the clock's speed enough to get Mycroft out of the Diogenes Club five minutes early—assuming the attempt on his life would be made when he exited. I judged that the six pounds I was carrying would come fairly close to gaining the time I required."

"You climbed all those stairs while lugging six pounds of dead weight?" MacKinnon asked.

"Actually, a little more than that."

"Blimey!" the policeman ejaculated. "And at your age."

Holmes ignored the criticism. "I had taken along," said he, "two copies of the 1908 *Chambers Dictionary*."

Two copies—now I understood the stop we had made at the library.

"Exactly, old fellow," said Holmes, following my line of thinking. "The dictionary's shipping weight is 3.3 pounds. I needed two. I trusted that I could borrow the one from your bookshelf, but I required another and hence our stop to see Lomax yesterday. I should say that he wasn't too keen on lending out a reference book like *Chambers*; but we've known each other for so long, you see, and when I told him a life hung in the balance—well, he reluctantly agreed."

"Very clever indeed," pronounced MacKinnon. "But just what exactly did you do with the books when you reached your destination?"

"I set them both on the tray atop the pendulum. I calculated that in the time remaining before Mycroft went off to his club, the books' combined weight would speed the clock up just enough to spare him. I knew that he set his watch by the striking of the chimes, and I reasoned that following the earlier time displayed by the clock in the tower would get him into—and subsequently out of—the Diogenes Club safely."

"Well played, Holmes," said I, bringing my hands together in applause. It was a beautiful plan—all the more magnificent because it worked.

"I have yet to retrieve the dictionaries, old fellow. They're up there still, I'm afraid. My apologies to you and Lomax."

I could only smile at my friend's concern.

"If I may ask," the Inspector said, "what made you assume the assault on your brother would occur on his way *out* and not when he entered? Wouldn't it have been more reasonable to detonate the thing when Mr Holmes went *in*? They could have planted the bomb at his favourite chair."

It was Mycroft who supplied the answer though it might just as easily have been his brother. "Put yourself in the shoes of the anarchist, Inspector. You would immediately see that the way *in* offers too many possibilities. Would I go directly to my chair? Was I meeting someone in the Strangers' Room? Might I stop in the lav? No, in dealing with my exit, not only were there fewer unknown locations, but also the timing was predictable."

"And just where was the bomb hidden?" I asked. "We did search the place."

"That I *can* tell you," grinned MacKinnon. "It was a devilishly clever hidey-hole, if you don't mind my saying so. That explains why the two of you missed it. The newspaper rack near the entrance is made of oak. The base is hollow, and that's where the timing device was put. But the really cunning part was the dynamite. One of the horizontal sticks on which the newspapers were draped had been replaced with a narrow tube, which contained two sticks of dynamite set in a row. Wires ran up from the end of the sticks and into the base."

"We didn't see them," said I, "and yet surely the wires would have been revealed earlier in the day when someone picked up a paper."

MacKinnon shook his head. "Possibly, Dr Watson, but not likely. The newspaper on the rack with the explosives was dated from last week. Very little interest in old news, I'm afraid."

"There's another important reason the bomb was placed in the foyer and not in a more social area, gentlemen," said my friend. "It was less likely to harm anyone else, which turned out to be the case. If one examines the killings for which the Assassination Bureau appear to be responsible, one must conclude that in their own twisted way they do not consider themselves barbarians. They—"

"Assassination Bureau?" MacKinnon interrupted.

"A criminal organisation we think might be behind all this," said Holmes.

"All *this*?" MacKinnon asked again. "All *what*?"

Clearly, neither Gregson nor Lestrade had shared with their colleagues the crucial information about the Assassination Bureau given to them by Jack London many years before.

"We don't know enough yet, Inspector," said Holmes. "We're not even certain such an organisation exists. But from what we've heard, we believe that they would never blow up a hall full of people to kill a single target. They claim a kind of distorted morality. They appear to believe that they are performing a public service by removing persons deemed detrimental to society."

"'*Deemed detrimental*—'?" MacKinnon repeated.

"Indeed. Such a philosophy would be destroyed if they eliminated the very members of the social order that they claim to be protecting—which is precisely what would have happened if that bomb tonight had detonated in the chamber filled with innocent members of the club."

Mycroft, who by now had regained much of his colour, furrowed his broad brow. "I realise it's early in your investigation, Mr MacKinnon," said he, "but is anyone yet suspected of this act?"

The Inspector turned his bowler again. "We think it was a woman."

"Hah!" Holmes ejaculated, his grey eyes flashing. "No doubt the very woman I accosted on the pavement—and that Scotland Yard have just released."

"Now, now, Mr Holmes. That's hard to say. The doorman reported an unidentified charwoman cleaning in the area of the newspapers this morning. Who she was and how she got in remains a mystery."

"I'll wager it's the same woman," said Holmes.

"Possibly, though, as you know, the woman we arrested earlier has yellow hair, and the char's was described as black."

Holmes, an expert in disguises, snorted derisively at the remark—as if hair colour by itself could be used as a distinction.

"What about the doorman at the club?" I asked. "Didn't *he* see her?"

"Maypoole?" said Mycroft. "He's too ancient to be definitive about anything he might have seen. Besides, I'm sure the woman changed her appearance well enough to fool people with far keener eyesight than his. What's more, she would have entered round back."

"Worse still," the Inspector added, "the calibre of the pistol taken from her this afternoon doesn't match the bullet we discovered in the window frame at the Morton-Watt shooting.' He cocked an eyebrow at Holmes. "Even if witnesses could confirm that she was working at the Old Bell Tavern the night of the murder, such testimony wouldn't confirm she was the second shooter."

"Agreed, MacKinnon," said Holmes. "And yet"—here he placed the fingertips of his hands together as he so often did when considering alternatives—"if she is at home, I would like to talk to her myself; if she is not, I would like to check her rooms. Perhaps there is something of value still to be found out there."

"We do have the address," said the Inspector preparing to rise.

"As do I," replied Holmes. He had already visited the place in his disguise as a dustman though he had not gone inside. The address itself was part of the information given to him by Shinwell Johnson.

"You understand," said MacKinnon as he placed the bowler on his head, "I don't have a warrant."

The three of us eyed him critically as he paused a moment. Then with an expression of resolve, he tapped the top of his derby. "There's a police motor outside. At the very least, it can take us to the building."

Holmes and I grabbed our hats and, assuring Mycroft we would keep him alerted, rushed out to the automobile. We had no thought of giving MacKinnon the chance to change his mind.

Chapter Nine

He who follows the fact cannot go astray,
while he who has no reverence for the fact wanders afar.
--Jack London
The Kempton-Wace Letters

Maisie Trilling lived in a woman's boarding house near the Westminster Bridge Road just south of the river and not far from Waterloo Station.

It was another moonless night; but thanks to the beams of our car's headlamps, once we entered Morley Street we could see that the first house, a three-storey structure of brown-brick and fronted by black railing, looked to be a respectable establishment. Thick vines of ivy covered the wall that faced the darkened side street; brightness spilled onto the front pavement from a large fanlight above the red outer-door.

Holmes indicated Miss Trilling's first-floor room on the ivy-covered wall. The room's only window was illuminated from a light that shone within.

At MacKinnon's order, the motor passed our destination and rolled to a stop some three houses beyond. With the headlamps turned off, we sat huddled in the car, but still close enough to the boarding house to see the front door. Intending to keep the police out of the business, Holmes and I exited the vehicle alone. Once we reached the entrance to the building, Holmes pulled the bell.

A tall, stern-faced woman opened the door part way. She wore her centre-parted black hair pulled straight back into a roll. Her dark dress was buttoned tight at the neck, and her defiant eyes suggested no quarter.

"Madam," said Holmes, "we would like to see Miss Maisie Trilling."

"This is an establishment for fine ladies," replied the woman tartly. "My guests do not entertain gentlemen here." Folding her arms, she barred the gate.

"Would you give her my card?" Holmes asked, fishing inside his coat for the item in question.

"No," said she, "I will *not*," and rudely closed the door.

Stymied, we retreated to the motor; and Holmes, after reporting to MacKinnon our lack of success, quickly conceived an alternate plan. The Inspector would identify himself to the landlady as the Metropolitan Police and ask to speak with Miss Trilling. Assuming he too would be put off, he would then engage the landlady in police business related to her boarder.

MacKinnon was a professional. Not only did he know which questions to ask but also how to threaten in response to a lack of cooperation. He would seek details concerning the length of Miss Trilling's stay, her supposed travel plans, the identities of any visitors she might have had, notable peculiarities in the letters she received—in short, anything that would preoccupy the woman for the few minutes Holmes and I required to climb the vines growing up the side of the building to Maisie Trilling's first-floor room. Apparently, Holmes intended to invent on the fly what we were to do when we encountered the woman at her window.

From our vantage point inside the police motor, we watched MacKinnon approach the red door. In the light produced as it opened, we could see him display his badge to the landlady and begin his diversionary action. Once he had engaged her, we sprang from the car and under cover of darkness dashed to the far side of the house. It was then we discovered the light in the window had been extinguished.

Then, just prior to grasping a thick branch in preparation for his climb, Holmes picked out from amidst the foliage a short strip of white lace, the kind of material found at the wrist of many a woman's dress.

"I don't like this, Watson," he whispered. "First the light; now the cloth. I fear that Maisie Trilling may have the heels of us."

I nodded to show I concurred.

"No doubt she witnessed our initial approach and made use of this escape route to fly. She's probably already boarded a train at Waterloo."

The ascent up the wall provided no obstacles; and in confirmation of Holmes' theory, we found the window wide open. Holmes climbed through, and I followed him into the small, darkened room.

"Do you smell it, Watson?" Holmes asked in a hushed voice.

"Strong tobacco?"

"Quite so," he whispered, "Makaroff cigarettes. Russian. We're in the right place."

Holmes rolled up a little rug he had found next to the bed and placed it at the foot of the door to prevent any light from reaching the outside hall. Only then did he push the electric wall-button. A small chandelier bathed the room in the brightness, and one could see immediately that the room was neatly accoutred. There stood a simple bed covered with a light-blue duvet, a bare desk with a green blotter, and an unadorned wooden dresser overlooked by an oak-framed mirror. In addition, a scuffed, brown-leather portmanteau stood just to the right of the door.

It was in vain that Holmes quickly searched the austere furniture and empty drawers for any personal items of the woman herself. Our attention thus turned to the suitcase. Too large to be carried through a window, let alone down the ivy, it had doubtlessly been left by the fleeing woman. We must have interrupted her just as she was about to make a more conventional exit. Obviously, she had concluded that the police were not yet finished with her.

Neither one of us was surprised that the suitcase turned out to be locked, but Sherlock Holmes—to whom most mechanisms presented no impediment—was not about to be checked by a mere baggage lock. Indeed, he had it open within seconds, and soon he was working his way through Miss Trilling's clothes, undergarments, and toilet articles with nary a suspicious item in sight.

"Hurry, Holmes," I whispered. "MacKinnon can't talk to that woman forever. She's the type who'll come up directly as soon as she's finished with him."

In response, Holmes lifted the suitcase over the bed and unceremoniously dumped the contents onto the duvet. He then ran his long, white fingers delicately across the inner cloth linings of the empty case.

From below, I could hear the front door close heavily. "Hurry," I pleaded.

Holmes tapped the back wall of the case. "Hullo," he muttered, "what have we here?" Peeling back the lining, he withdrew from a false bottom a small book with dark-green covers.

"Well, well," said he softly as he eyed the gilt-lettered title. "Here's an irony, indeed."

Holding the volume aloft, he whispered, "*The Secret Agent,* a novel by my old friend Joseph Conrad, which I have read with great interest."

Thanks to Lomax at the London Library, the book was familiar to me as well. It offers a fictional account of the very real bombing of the Greenwich Royal Observatory in 1894. That fiendish plot played a role in Holmes' dealings with the American novelist Stephen Crane, about whom I have already written. It was during that investigation, the account of which I titled "Sherlock Holmes and the Baron of Brede Place", that I too had met Mr Conrad.

"It does seem appropriate," Holmes observed, "for an assassin to be reading the tale of an infernal device. 'Coals to Newcastle,' and yet . . . ." As he spoke, he riffled the pages; and a small piece of paper, seemingly a bookmarker, fluttered to the floor.

Suddenly, the beat of determined footsteps sounded on the stairs.

Holmes snatched up the scrap. "Come!" was all he said— all he *needed* to say—before climbing out the window. I required no words of encouragement to follow him; and leaving the contents of the suitcase splayed across the bed, we made our way to the ground.

"Go!" MacKinnon commanded the driver as we threw ourselves into the rear seats of the police motor.

As the car lurched forward, Holmes held up the tiny piece of paper. "It's a list of four names," he said triumphantly as we rumbled down the Westminster Bridge Road. "A kill-list, I should judge."

"An *illegally-procured* kill-list," MacKinnon felt compelled to remind us.

"Two of the names are not surprising," Holmes continued, "Charles Morton-Watt and Mycroft Holmes. But there are two new names, gentlemen, names that have not yet appeared in connection with this murderous syndicate—at least, not as targets. One is Jack London, the American writer who brought this nefarious organisation to our attention in the first place."

"Why might someone approach the Bureau with the need to murder *him*?" I asked.

"Perhaps it's the Bureau themselves who want him eliminated. Perhaps, they've finally figured out in how much danger he's placed them."

I agreed. I could not imagine anyone disturbed enough by London's writings to come to the Assassination Bureau seeking the man's demise. Revenge, however, was a different matter. The Bureau might well have wanted to eliminate the agent of its exposure.

"Whose is the last name on the list?" MacKinnon wanted to know. "Whoever it is, we'll have to notify him as soon as possible."

"An Austrian, Inspector. The Archduke Franz Ferdinand. Heir to the throne of the Austro-Hungarian Empire."

"The Austro-Hungarian Empire," MacKinnon muttered, pulling on his moustache. "Serbia's part of that, isn't it?" he offered. "That's where Maisie Tilling said she was off to when she defended the right to possess her pistol."

Though the name of Franz Josef, the Austrian emperor, was known to me, I confessed to never having heard of the archduke. And yet he was a member of the royal family.

"No doubt this Franz Ferdinand is a noble gentleman," said I. "To be sure, there must be malcontents who are unhappy with their government, but it seems unreasonable to hold responsible a lone man who's not yet the ruler of the land."

"Quite so, Watson. And yet we must alert his Highness to the intent of the Assassination Bureau. Whatever the motivation, I have little doubt that the murder of such a prominent figure could well spark a large-scale war."

The political rumblings all over Europe were well known at the time, and yet I could not fathom how the death of a single individual might lead to any large-scale conflagration. Still, Holmes was correct about the need for urgency. We did have to warn the man.

"All this political talk may be interesting," said MacKinnon, "but in light of this list, it is the more practical matter that concerns me—finding Maisie Trilling."

"Let us hope you are successful in your search, Inspector," said Holmes. A moment later he added *sotto voce:* "But I doubt you will be."

I would rather be the man whose house was burned,
than the man who burned it.
--Jack London (attributed)

As Sherlock Holmes had predicted, no arrest was ever made of the woman called Maisie Trilling. Despite our lingering suspicions that she was, in fact, Grunya, the daughter of the Russian who supposedly headed the Assassination Bureau, no one to our knowledge has seen her since—at least, not in England.

As for Jack London, I received a typed letter from him the following summer. I showed it to Holmes, of course; and I reproduce it here as the final correspondence the man ever shared with us:

```
                           Beauty Ranch
                           Sonoma County
                           Sep 3, 1913.


Dear Mr. Holmes and Dr. Watson: --
     I don't know if you've heard the terrible
news from here.  I'm so miserable I still can't
bear to work at my desk, so I'm sitting up in bed
to write.  But write I must, for since the tragedy
is so much a part of the twisted story we've been
following together all these years, I feel that you
should know what's happened.
```

147

About a week ago, Wolf House, the home of my
dreams--almost completed but not yet moved into--
was burned to the ground. I have yet to overcome
the unrelenting grief and horrific shock this
monumental tragedy has brought upon me.

I helped design it, gentlemen, a twenty-six-
room mansion not far from our present ranch. It
was an artistic creation--my ideal of utility and
beauty fused into one. All the building material
was local--stone walls, volcanic rock, redwood
rafters, Spanish tiles--everything from around here
to make the house look rustic and handsome. It was
shaped like a U and had a concrete reflecting pool
in the center that I was planning to fill with
mountain bass and trout and maybe even swim right
along with them. My second-floor study, the place
where I planned to do all my writing, was set apart
from the rest of the house. It was to be my
retreat.

But then, just over a week ago, on the night
of August 22, the place was destroyed--gutted--
ruined--by fire. Officials tell me the blaze
started around midnight. And because the house was
located in a hollow, the fire went unnoticed until
the sky turned red and people all over the
countryside could see the glow. By the time my
wife Charmian and I were awakened and got out to

the place, it was too late. With no water to fight the blaze, the house was gone in three hours.

Charmian thinks I've behaved like a stoic, but I can assure you that I shed real tears. It wasn't just that it was my house. It was appreciated by everybody who saw it. The Oakland paper called it a "forest castle," and a famous architect said it was "the most beautiful house in America." But mainly it was mine, and I'm convinced its destruction was a message sent by forces out to get me. My chief contractor was supposed to inspect the house every evening to be sure all was in order, but would you believe that for whatever the reason there was no one watching the property that night in particular? Somebody fired the place. I just know it.

What's more, I'm not the only one who thinks so. Charmian said she couldn't put a name on them, but she believes the place was torched by my enemies. Some think that maybe my brother-in-law played a role. After all, my sister is divorcing him, and on the day of the fire he was angry enough to be waving a gun around, and I had to throw him out.

Others blame it on farmers who fear a Socialist moving in—me! I'd have laughed it off if I could because--ironically enough--suspicion also falls on radical anarchists and Socialist agents who are claiming I built a rich man's castle on the backs of the workingman. On the backs of the workingman! Hell, I paid workingmen with my own wages to build the place! And while we're looking for suspects, let's not forget the character claiming to be me who's running around the country and signing his checks with my name.

But empty charges all, gentlemen--I'm sure you'll agree. I'm writing to you both because only the three of us know who's really behind this evil. The Assassination Bureau is out to get me, and I fear the house is only the start. It's why I'm not asking for any sort of investigation into the cause of the fire. Let sleeping dogs lie. Charmian and I were scheduled to move in the day after the place burned down, but--who knows?--maybe they thought I was already inside. I've talked a little about rebuilding. But I can't for the life of me imagine spending the time to do it again. Why, it takes 18 months just to cure the redwood! And what's the point anyhow if that damned organization keeps coming after me?

$80,000 lost in the inferno. That's what the house cost. I've taken to calling it a "beautiful fire" in the sense that there was so much destruction of beauty. All that's left now is the

skeleton of the structure. I look into the
blackness of the ruins and see my future. Next time
it might not only be a house they eliminate--

Jack London

Wolf House was never rebuilt, and three years after the conflagration Jack London was dead. Just as questions haunted the destruction of the building, so suspicions swirled round the death of its owner.

According to the authorities, Jack London died from an overdose of morphine. But who could be certain of the details? He had been taking the drug for medicinal reasons, so one may rightly wonder if his death had simply been a terrible accident. And yet one may also ask whether the overdose had been intentional? Had he committed suicide? Or, as London himself had indirectly predicted, had someone entered his room and poisoned him with the drug? Recalling the Assassination Bureau's list of targets, I suspect the latter.

Much has already been written of the murder of the heir to the Austro-Hungarian throne less than a year later. In spite of the warnings offered by Holmes, Archduke Franz Ferdinand was shot dead in his automobile in Sarajevo. As my friend had accurately foreseen, the consequences of the Archduke's untimely death put into play the violent forces that erupted in August of 1914 into the conflagration we now call the Great War.

Like the analyses of so many other assassins over the years, countless theories have been offered about the Archduke's killer and his confederates. It is believed that Gavrilo Princip, the shooter, most probably had connections with one or more clandestine organisations. The notorious Black Hand and even Gorgianno's Red Circle are but two of many accused. Those of us familiar with the Assassination Bureau's self-righteous calling, however—not to mention the rumours of a Russian young lady with curly black hair having been seen with Princip—may draw other conclusions.

As we all know, following the entry of the United States into the fray, the Great War eventually ended with the defeat of Germany. Thanks to America's resulting emergence as a world power, there are many prognosticators who believe the new century will be dominated by the United States. A peaceful world should indeed be the consequence of so terrible a conflict. No less an observer than Bertie Wells, my old friend from Brede Place, referred to the titanic struggle as "the war to end war".

Those self-proclaimed predictors of peace, however, remain ignorant of an important consideration. Despite the resolution of the international hostilities—or, perhaps, because of it—there is a small group, myself included, who recognise a burgeoning America as fertile soil for the continued growth of the Assassination Bureau.

Though such views may continue to remain speculative, Jack London correctly understood that even the most modest of hints regarding the existence of so deadly an organisation continues to fascinate people. In his own day, it was London's appreciation of such interest that served as the catalyst for beginning his own novel about the group. Today, close to twenty years after London put away his unfinished manuscript, crime writers who also understand the appeal still toy with the idea of completing it. I feel certain that someday an author will. For that matter, perhaps in the not too distant future, a brave cinema company will produce a film of the tale.

One final word remains to be said. The Great War ended more than ten years ago. Yet even I, a mere chronicler of the events surrounding the evil group thought to have set it off, do not feel immune. Whether the organisation is real or not, I worry none the less that its mercenaries may be coming for me. Such is the unspoken power of the Assassination Bureau. I have never forgot the incident of the car that had almost run me down. Innocent though I am, even now I look over my shoulder with trepidation whenever I hear at my back the clatter of crisp footfalls on the pavement or the echoes of heavy boots in a hallway—especially if the steps seem to be hurrying in my direction.

THE END

Suggested Reading from the Editor

To supplement Dr. Watson's narrative, interested readers should obviously begin with Jack London's unfinished novel, *The Assassination Bureau, Ltd.* It turns out that Watson was correct on two counts related to the book.

First, another author actually did complete the work. In 1963, American mystery writer Robert L. Fish composed the final third of *The Assassination Bureau, Ltd.* Although Fish could have followed the various suggestions left by both London and London's widow Charmian (their notes appear in the Penguin edition), he composed his own conclusion. It should be emphasised, however, that none of the three options presents the ominous implications raised by Watson in *The Outrage at the Diogenes Club*.

Watson also accurately predicted that London's novel would interest the movie industry. The film version of *The Assassination Bureau* appeared in 1969 starring Diana Rigg and Oliver Reed. It too, however, lacks the gravitas with which Watson rightly approached the subject. As for the product of Jack London's stay in England back in 1903, one should consult *The People of the Abyss*, his account of the debilitating conditions faced by the poor in London's East End at the start of the twentieth century.

Additional information related to Dr. Watson's narrative may be found in Dale L. Walker's *Jack London and Conan Doyle: A Literary Kinship.* Of particular interest is the chapter with the Holmesian title, "The Singular Adventure of Hal Lewis's Plots." For the history of the assassination attempt on Theodore Roosevelt, Gerard Helferich's *Theodore Roosevelt and the Assassin: Madness, Vengeance, and the Campaign of 1912* offers a detailed report. And, of course, *The Seventh Bullet*, Dr. Watson's account (which I edited) of Sherlock Holmes' investigation into the murder of David Graham Phillips, provides additional facts about that assassination in particular.

For information regarding what is now called the Elizabeth Tower in the palace of Westminster, the Houses of Parliament have published *Big Ben and the Elizabeth Tower*, a most useful guide full of technological, historical, and anecdotal material as well as wonderful illustrations, including a fold-out cover, that depict the locations visited by Sherlock Holmes in his attempts to protect his brother.

It goes without saying that, since each of the volumes mentioned above was published before the recent discovery of this latest manuscript by Dr. Watson, none of them makes reference to any of the new details revealed in *The Outrage at the Diogenes Club.*

Also from Daniel D. Victor

The American Literati Series

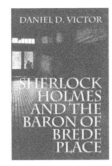

The Final Page of Baker Street
The Baron of Brede Place
Seventeen Minutes To Baker Street

"The really amazing thing about this book [*The Final Page of Baker Street*] is the author's ability to call up the 'essence' of both the Baker Street 'digs' of Holmes and Watson as well as that of the 'mean streets' of Marlowe's Los Angeles. Although none of the action takes place in either place, Holmes and Watson share a sense of camaraderie and self-confidence in facing threats and problems that also pervades many of the later tales in the Canon. Following their conversations and banter is a return to Edwardian England and its certainties and hope for the future. This is definitely the world before The Great War."

Philip K Jones

www.mxpublishing.com

Also from MX Publishing

MX Publishing is the world's largest specialist Sherlock Holmes publisher, with over a hundred titles and fifty authors creating the latest in Sherlock Holmes fiction and non-fiction.

From traditional short stories and novels to travel guides and quiz books, MX Publishing cater for all Holmes fans.

The collection includes leading titles such as *Benedict Cumberbatch In Transition* and *The Norwood Author* which won the 2011 Howlett Award (Sherlock Holmes Book of the Year).

MX Publishing also has one of the largest communities of Holmes fans on <u>Facebook</u> with regular contributions from dozens of authors.

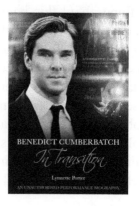

<u>www.mxpublishing.com</u>

Also from MX Publishing

 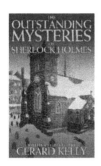 

Our bestselling books are our short story collections;

'Lost Stories of Sherlock Holmes' , 'The Outstanding Mysteries of Sherlock Holmes', The Papers of Sherlock Holmes Volume 1 and 2, 'Untold Adventures of Sherlock Holmes' (and the sequel 'Studies in Legacy) and 'Sherlock Holmes in Pursuit', 'The Cotswold Werewolf and Other Stories of Sherlock Holmes' – and many more......

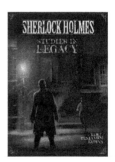  

www.mxpublishing.com

Also from MX Publishing

"Phil Growick's, 'The Secret Journal of Dr Watson', is an adventure which takes place in the latter part of Holmes and Watson's lives. They are entrusted by HM Government (although not officially) and the King no less to undertake a rescue mission to save the Romanovs, Russia's Royal family from a grisly end at the hand of the Bolsheviks. There is a wealth of detail in the story but not so much as would detract us from the enjoyment of the story. Espionage, counter-espionage, the ace of spies himself, double-agents, double-crossers...all these flit across the pages in a realistic and exciting way. All the characters are extremely well-drawn and Mr Growick, most importantly, does not falter with a very good ear for Holmesian dialogue indeed. Highly recommended. A five-star effort."

The Baker Street Society

www.mxpublishing.com

Also from MX Publishing

The Missing Authors Series

Sherlock Holmes and The Adventure of The Grinning Cat

Sherlock Holmes and The Nautilus Adventure

Sherlock Holmes and The Round Table Adventure

"Joseph Svec, III is brilliant in entwining two endearing and enduring classics of literature, blending the factual with the fantastical; the playful with the pensive; and the mischievous with the mysterious. We shall, all of us young and old, benefit with a cup of tea, a tranquil afternoon, and a copy of Sherlock Holmes, The Adventure of the Grinning Cat."

Amador County Holmes Hounds Sherlockian Society

www.mxpublishing.com

Also from MX Publishing

The Detective and The Woman Series

The Detective and The Woman
The Detective, The Woman and The Winking Tree
The Detective, The Woman and The Silent Hive

"The book is entertaining, puzzling and a lot of fun. I believe the author has hit on the only type of long-term relationship possible for Sherlock Holmes and Irene Adler. The details of the narrative only add force to the romantic defects we expect in both of them and their growth and development are truly marvelous to watch. This is not a love story. Instead, it is a coming-of-age tale starring two of our favorite characters."

Philip K Jones

www.mxpublishing.com

Milton Keynes UK
Ingram Content Group UK Ltd.
UKHW040735121124
2770UKWH00030B/139